GETTING INTO
MANIFESTATION ZONE

GETTING INTO MANIFESTATION ZONE

A Radical Way To Manifest 24/7

RICHARD DOTTS

TABLE OF CONTENTS

CHAPTER ONE

IS THERE A
MANIFESTATION ZONE?

Is there a sacred manifestation zone—a place where we can move into and have all our deepest desires automatically come true?

If such a place exists, where do we find it? How do we get there in the first place? It turns out that the way to get there is easier than you think.

It is great to be back at my writing desk working on this brand new book. I have not been writing for a while in light of the major changes in my life. For the past few months, I have been busy with a major relocation opportunity and several new projects that manifested in my own life. Looking back, these opportunities would not have been opened up for the "old" Richard, the version of me that was always fearful, skeptical, and worried about the future. However, because I made a deliberate attempt to put these Universal principles into action and to let go of my fear-based beliefs, the Universe responded in the most brilliant of ways. Life continues to unfold beautifully for me every single day as I continue to take things one step at a time, knowing that all is well, and that I am taken care of—every single step along the way.

Were there moments where I worried that my writing was lagging behind and that I was letting my readers down? Definitely—but I have also learned through my firsthand application of these Universal Laws, that worrying (for whatever reason at all) is futile and counterproductive. Any time we worry about something, we are building up negative energy that goes on to create our (future) physical reality. With that realization, I gently let my worrying thoughts go. I refused to feel guilty about not writing or letting my readers down. I let go of all my expectations about what I was *supposed* to do as an author, and just let things *be*. I knew that if I was relaxed enough, then source energy could flow through me easily and I would know intuitively when I needed to work on my next book.

It turns out that I did not have to wait for long. A few weeks after wondering what I would write about next, the premise for this book came into my mind. Until today, I remain convinced that the idea for this series of manifestation books is divinely inspired. Of course, I would not go as far to say that these books are channeled, but the bulk of this material (which has spanned over twenty books so far) definitely comes from a wiser, all-knowing part of myself. As I write, I feel myself relaxing into and melding with a greater, all-encompassing consciousness that is larger than my physical presence in this world. As the words flow effortlessly from my fingertips onto the screen, I do very little censoring or editing. I may occasionally rewrite a sentence for clarity (and my editor does a great job at cleaning up the text, thank you!), but that is about as far as I would go in rewriting or restructuring any of this material. Most of the time, I let whatever words that need to be said reveal themselves on these blank pages with very little planning. The end result always takes me by surprise. What emerges is an overarching structure and flow to the work that is better than anything I thought I could have conceived. My readers seem to pick up on this too, and feel themselves gently getting into the Universal flow as they read. That's because I do not pretend to be someone else when I write. By not censoring the words and ideas that come up (to sound more intelligent, for example), I am free to simply be myself.

Some people would consider my writing process mystical, or perhaps even a little creepy. "How is it that Richard gets words to flow so effortlessly onto the pages, and how is it that he writes so many books without much physical effort? It's almost unfair!" Indeed, mankind has a tendency to attribute inexplicable phenomenon to hidden or dark forces. That is why we tend to be so fearful of the unknown. Much of the creative process itself is invisible, and happens below the threshold of our waking consciousness. Take for example a painter at work, her hands moving skillfully across the canvas, as she has done thousands of times. She knows exactly the right amount of force to apply, the angle of the brush making contact with the paper, and the right amount of colors to mix in order to achieve the desired end result. The entire process does not require conscious intervention from her. But—when you force her to break it down into conscious steps, the creative flow gets broken. She may give you an after-the-fact rationalization of why she is using her brush a certain way, but she will never be able to properly explain the entire creative process from start to finish.

For example, where does she find her inspiration? How does she turn her ideas into physical (observable) reality on the canvas? Each of these remain largely unknown and unobservable. They are intuitive skills that are gradually picked up by a skilled craftsman as he immerses himself in his craft. It is the same with any kind of artistic expression, be it singing, drawing, painting, or writing.

It is the same with physical manifestations as well. Your life is an artistic expression of your own creativity. Much of this creative process has remained under the threshold of your waking consciousness. Much of what we can observe are the tangible results *after* they have manifested—the physical objects such as houses, cars, relationships, and external results. However, the physical world is only a very small part of the picture, just as the painter would tell you that the final drawing represents only a small part of the story which she wants to tell. There is so much more to a painting than just the specks of color you see on the canvas. The creative process actually extends beyond the canvas, and begins in the consciousness of the painter. *A Course in Miracles* says, "There is no point in trying to change the world. It is incapable of change because it is merely an effect."

In the same way, the words which you are reading right now represent only a small part of what I am trying to convey, not merely the starting point. These words are the end result of the creative process of my writing, but they do not tell the whole story. Before these words flowed out of my mind and onto these pages, they were already ruminating somewhere in my consciousness. They were already assembled and waiting to be written down as ideas. And what brought those ideas to their holding place? What organized those ideas and held them in place? It is the creative, intelligent energy that flows through each and every one of us. Some cultures call it *life force* or *divine substance*. It is this divine substance that flows through and permeates everything.

Here's where it gets even more exciting: What does this formless, intelligent substance respond to? **It responds to our deepest intentions, thoughts and feelings.** This divine substance permeating the whole of the Universe responds instantly to the slightest of our inner thoughts, whether we like it or not. We are literally made up of this formless substance, and at one with this Universal energy at all times. We can never be separate from it, which is really a good thing!

Let's backtrack a little, and take a look at my writing process and its greater significance: A few paragraphs ago, I told you that these words seemed to flow through me effortlessly onto these pages, in the same way a painting "flows through" the painter. Before a book is written or a painting is painted however, it is held in some kind of a "holding place" in our inner consciousness, waiting to be expressed creatively, and rendered into tangible physical form. But what causes this collection of ideas to be assembled in the first place? That's right—none other than the earlier intentions planted by the writer or painter! The mere *intention* was what set in motion the chain of events to come, aided along by the natural laws of the Universe.

So while one could say a particular physical manifestation would not have occurred without the Universe, it is just as equally valid to say that the Universe would not exist if not for the myriad of our intentions and thoughts. Otherwise, the whole Universe would just be a single, formless state. It is our thoughts and intentions which move the Universe along, resulting in our ever-growing expansion. This is what Abraham-Hicks mean by being at the cutting-edge of thought. The Universe advances with each new intention and each new manifestation that results from us.

When you view the Universe in this manner, you start appreciating your role as a powerful creator of your own physical reality, along with all the other co-creators in your life. This is why spiritual teachers often teach that there is no separation between us and the Universe, and that we are literally *at one* with everything around us. We are both the creators and the products of our creation. At the same time, we are made up of the same formless energy that creates worlds, so we are actually everything at once—the creators, the creative force in motion, and the created. This is an extremely powerful realization to hold in your consciousness.

This is also what makes the Taoist yin-yang symbol so profound. More than just a clever piece of artwork, the yin and yang symbol portrays a sense of complete balance. Just as shadows cannot exist without light, and black cannot exist without white, the Universe cannot exist without you. You cannot exist independently from the Universe. That's not because you are dependent *on* the Universe, but because you *are* the Universe. You are literally one *with* the Universe.

If we are all powerful creators at the core of our own being, inseparable from this creative life force that flows through us...then why stop at our current circumstances? If we are all unlimited beings, why not create an unlimited life in all areas? The preceding discussion brings me to the powerful premise for this next book, which you are now holding in your hands. It is also the blossoming of an intention that I planted several weeks ago which helped set everything into motion, leading to the publication of this book. While I feel I have said almost everything possible on the subject of manifestations, the unlimited Universe has shown me there is something more. After all, it is our thoughts and intentions that will move our consciousness forward. The Universe is now nudging me to tell you to not stop here, and settle for your current circumstances.

Why acknowledge that you are an "unlimited being" and then settle for lack, unhappiness, or minor improvements in circumstances on the other hand? Why read all these self-help books and then still have to deal with some of the grievances in your own life? The Universe has been telling me that I can go all out to create my life in whatever way I want through a series of powerful lessons...and so can you.

I am excited about what this book brings for you. Whether you are a new or familiar reader of my works, it is going to push the boundaries of your current notions of manifestation from where we left off in my previous works. We are going to explore new techniques, new ways of thinking, and new possibilities. Together, we are going to take thought (and our collective consciousness) beyond where it has gone before.

You are going to learn why this concept of balance—so brilliantly portrayed by the yin-yang symbol—is critical to manifesting the conditions which you desire in your daily life. I am excited to share the new practice of 24/7 manifestations—which is all about moving into a special "manifestation zone" where all your deepest desires automatically come true—and how you can stay there! You'll learn how being inside this manifestation zone results in spontaneous manifestations, without you having to strain or struggle to create the desired outer circumstances in your life. You will see why this new way of living automatically clears up many of your perceived outer problems and struggles, and why it is so much easier than trying some of the more traditional techniques you have been taught.

It is going to be wild ride down the rabbit hole of the Universe! Let's begin...

CHAPTER TWO

WHY SETTLE FOR
ANYTHING LESS?

How many times have you said to yourself, "My life is already pretty good, perhaps I should not ask for too much." This is a common pitfall that many students of this metaphysical material often fall into. They apply the techniques, see a few improvements in their lives, and then forget all about applying these principles on a consistent basis. As old belief patterns and habits die hard, they soon find themselves regressing back into their former selves.

I used to be like this as well. I would apply the techniques, get some promising results, and then promptly go back to my old ways of thinking and acting, out of the sheer force of habit. I would usually stop when I thought I had made enough progress. This is usually what happens when you take a piecemeal approach to spiritual manifestations, when you try to apply certain techniques to "patch" up the areas in your life that need mending. The patched up areas just don't seem to hold up very well, or for very long.

I have often taught that the secret behind effective manifestations lies in not taking a Band-Aid approach to life. Stop seeing your life (and yourself) as something broken that needs to be fixed. Things may *seem* so on a physical level, and it may even be true that many things are not to your liking in your physical reality right now. However, beneath all of that, just below the threshold of your physical awareness, is the spiritual perfection of everything. This may be difficult for you to accept at this time (especially when faced with all the unfulfilled desires and challenges in your life), but stay with me and this truth will become clearer as we progress through the book.

The first step is to truly acknowledge and make peace with these "unwanted bits" of your life. They are here now in your physical reality, no matter what. Sure, you may not welcome the physical or emotional pain you feel, but it is here. You may not welcome the financial lack that you are experiencing, but it is here. Stop fighting it! Acknowledge that it is here and make peace with it. Within the peace and stillness lies an amazing amount of power which you can draw upon. This first step will bring you considerable peace and power over the situation. Some people spend all their lives fighting reality and denying that the reality is the way it currently is. The good news is that just because it is here *now*, doesn't mean it is here *to stay*. Because physical reality is so malleable, outer circumstances can be easily changed once we allow them to. First, we must learn how to focus our energies in the right manner—not on denial, but on advancement.

I spent more than ten years of my life resisting the fact that I had issues with financial lack. On a certain level, I was afraid to acknowledge my situation because I thought that doing so would welcome more of the same circumstances into my own life. I was also an avid student of all these self-help and spiritual materials, and I mistakenly thought that I would "attract" more of the same if I made peace with my situation. I was also embarrassed to let others know that I had not been successful at applying this material for myself!

However, making peace is not the same as setting an intention *for* something. Making peace means that you acknowledge it is there and nothing more. Peace in itself (as I've written in my previous books) is a neutral emotion that does nothing and goes nowhere. By making peace with your current situation, you are not creating more of the unwanted situation in your own life. Instead, what you are doing is freeing up all that mental energy which you have previously used to deny the situation day in and day out. All of this mental energy and focus can now be put to good use—towards creating a more desired reality.

Now that something unwanted is here in your life and you have acknowledged it, what steps can you take to replace this unwanted reality with a more desired version? Where do we go from here?

If you observe people who struggle with addictions, what is the first thing they usually say? "I do not have a problem!" That's right—to these individuals, they do not think they have an issue, but everyone around them can clearly see the havoc the addiction wreaks in their own lives. Saying "Yes, I do have an issue here," will be a more powerful stance than denying that the problem exists. Similarly, we can be blind to the issues that exist in our own lives.

One easy way to tell where the issue lies is by looking at the areas of our lives that result in the most negative emotions. For example, I used to be constantly worried about having not enough money. Therefore, my financial situation brought me the most negative feelings. Yet at the same time, I was vehemently trying to deny that there was an issue in that area of my life! Do you see the connection now? You may deny that a particular undesired situation exists, but your constant negative emotions will alert you to the fact that something needs to be changed. Your negative emotions are actually important signals for growth and change.

Another way to convince ourselves that everything is alright is to say, "My life is already pretty good, perhaps I should not ask for too much." Sound familiar? That is another way of limiting your own potential by not going all out and experiencing all this Universal goodness for yourself. Why shortchange yourself by accepting even *some* suffering in your life? You are an unlimited being. Your life can be one hundred percent happy and completely fulfilled in all areas. The Universe gives you everything you can possibly ask for, and I would not settle for anything less!

Why is it so difficult for us to accept the notion that life can be perfect in all areas? I think there are two main reasons. The first reason stems from social and cultural conditioning. We have been made to believe that man is not perfect, and that only God represents perfection. We have been asked by our parents from a young age to "manage our expectations" so as not to be disappointed when things do not work out—to expect challenges and problems in our own lives. We have been culturally conditioned, over and over again with sayings such as, "Life is not a bed of roses," or "What doesn't kill you makes you stronger." All of these beliefs are so deeply ingrained within our belief system that we are unable to recognize our perfect, divine nature. Add on to that, the guilt or shame we feel from thinking of ourselves as perfect beings. All of this keeps us from asking for a perfect life!

The second reason stems from a lack of understanding of these Universal Laws. As I mentioned in the previous chapter, much of the creative process remains hidden beneath the surface of our conscious awareness. What we can observe is merely the physical end result of our creations. This means that most people are not familiar with these Universal Laws, and as a result, they fear what they do not know. Only with thorough study and observation can one uncover the secrets of the Universe.

There was a time in my life when I thought I was going to die because I was feeling so good and things were going so well. Yet another cultural aphorism for this is, "It felt so good...I thought I had died and gone to heaven!"

It is absolutely absurd, if you think about it. Why would we equate physical death (something feared and unwanted in our society) with feeling good? What can't feeling good be associated with even better things to come in our lives? Ever since I realized the absurdity of this social conditioning at work, I have changed my beliefs to: "There is no limit to how good I can feel. Every day I feel better and better." This is a good affirmation to start with.

So what does all of this teach us? First, it tells us that a huge chunk of life is arbitrary and based on absurd rules that have been embedded in our consciousness over time. We have come to accept certain cultural sayings and beliefs as Universal truths, when in fact we can just as easily believe in something else. Second, unless one is a conscientious student of these Universal Laws, we will forever be living and operating based on the mistaken beliefs of other people. These are the beliefs we have unknowingly accepted from our parents, friends, teachers, or the authority figures in our own lives, who in turn accepted them from their parents, friends, and teachers in their lives. It is time to question these beliefs and create a new reality for ourselves.

The main reason why I was nudged to write this book (resulting in me asking the Universe for some guidance, which it gladly provided) was because I observed many of my readers going just part of the way in their exploration of this material. For example, they may have read one of my books such as *Your Greatest Gift*, accept the *premise* that they are powerful creators, and then settle for less than desirable results in some areas of their lives. When I say you can use these teachings to create anything you want in life, I really do mean *anything*. There is no limit to what you can manifest.

I can say this unequivocally because I have been down this path myself. I have held myself back before, afraid of going all out and creating the life that I desired. I accepted five thousand dollars' worth of results when I really wanted to ask for twenty thousand. I was willing to live with unhappiness in certain areas of my life, because I thought these spiritual techniques would not apply to them all.

Here is where I can tell you that these spiritual principles do apply to *all* areas of your life. You are a multi-dimensional being (as Seth puts it) and there is not a single dimension of your consciousness that remains outside the reach of these Universal Laws. They can, and do work for everything, if you take the effort necessary to work them. You do not have to live with physical grievances, minor inconveniences, or certain undesirable aspects of your life…everything can be shaped and changed in an instant!

It boils down to the only question being whether you *want* to. Remember that above all of this, there exists an element of free will and personal choice. You are free to create reality in any way you want, even in a way that traps you and makes you immensely unhappy. The Universe (which is actually you) does not interfere in any of it. Therefore, you can choose to accept partial results and go halfway, or you can choose to lead an unlimited life and go all out. The Universe will react accordingly regardless of which choice you make. Louise Hay has a great analogy for this. She teaches that some people go to the abundant ocean with a spoon, others go with a bucket. The ocean of life is unlimited, and so is your consciousness. Life will give you whatever you can ask for, because this life force has never been separate from you.

As we round up this chapter, I would like you to take a piece of paper and write down the things or situations which you have been denying in your own life. No one else is going to read what goes on this piece of paper but yourself, so you can be honest here. You can shred it or burn it when you are done—but I want you to write it down, because then, your ego mind can't do its thing and attempt to convince you that the situation does not exist. What issues have you been denying till now? If nothing comes up, look at areas of your life which have been a constant source of negative feelings or emotions. Write those areas down. It may be that you have nothing at all, but it is very rare to come across someone who has totally worked through all their issues. Be persistent at it and honest with yourself.

For each of the issues you have written on the paper, say out loud, "I have ___," and notice how you feel. Do this exercise in a place where you feel totally safe and where you know you will not be overheard. I like to do it when I'm alone in my car. For example, if you want to work with your issues of financial lack, say, "I have not enough money," and notice how that feels. Once again, do not be worried that making such a statement will instantly cause you to "attract" undesired circumstances into your life. You are making this statement to acknowledge and make peace with something you have been denying for the longest time. Denying something involves considerable negative energy, which in fact perpetuates and attracts more of the same situation in your reality. In contrary, making peace with a situation and transmuting the negative energy to peace diffuses the situation. You are no longer holding an emotionally attractive charge. This means you are beginning to soften reality the way it is, and stop perpetuating more of the unwanted situation.

Say this little statement five or ten times and notice how your energy changes as you speak the words out loud. Repeat the statement until your negative emotions have been transformed into a sense of inner calmness and peace. Some relief is what we are looking for here. If you are struggling with an addiction which you have been denying for the longest time, say "I am addicted to ___." Feel the sense of disgust, embarrassment, shame, guilt, or sadness that comes up. Let it flow freely. You are safe here, in the privacy of your own inner sanctuary. Repeat this five, ten, twenty, or even fifty times in the privacy of your own room or automobile. There is no need to count, just repeat the statement out loud until you feel a shift in your own energy to a sense of peacefulness. It is alright to let the tears flow freely as you do this exercise, as it represents a releasing of negative resistance which will be immensely helpful. The key is to notice how your energy changes as you acknowledge your current situation.

You may experience a strong sense of denial or disconnect the first few times you say the statement. Gradually, it may slowly turn into feelings of sadness as you come face-to-face and become connected with your current reality, which you have avoided for quite some time. As you continue to repeat the statement, you may find a newfound sense of calmness and peace wash over you. For the first time in your life, you realize that this is just a temporary condition and nothing else. Even *this* can be changed, and you have taken the first step towards creating positive results. The wonderful thing about this exercise is that you can stop right here and wonderful things will begin to take their own course. Through one simple exercise, you have let go of years of negative feelings and have freed up much of your mental energies, which can now be put toward more productive use. So even if you were to stop here—with no expectations, subtle physical changes will go on to happen in your life.

If you would like to go further, ask yourself whether you would like to change each of the issues which you have written down on paper. Go down the list and ask whether it is something you should work on at this time. Let the answer come to you naturally. We are not looking for an intellectual answer here, but something that comes from your deepest self. Sometimes it may be a yes, and at other times it may be a no. I encourage you to work on the areas that you receive a "yes" for at this time, and leave the rest for a more appropriate time. The Universe will let you know when the time is right. Even if you receive a "no," it does not mean that the unwanted situation is permanent in your life, or that it is unresolvable.

Remember that Universal perfection is the foundation of everything. Our limited human perspectives cannot fully grasp the perfection of things at a single point in time. Know that the Universe is always guiding you towards your highest good. This means letting the Universe do its job when it needs to.

How does all this tie into the art of manifestations? When you finally make peace with everything in your life, you gently dissolve the negative blocks and resistances which you have unknowingly held on to for a long time. These blocks occupy much of your conscious awareness, which makes it difficult for you to focus on creating a more desired reality. Now that these blocks are gone, you are free from the habits and mind chatter that have held you back in the past. In the next chapter, we are going to talk about the structure of the Universe and how a sense of balance is the key in manifesting twenty-four hours a day, every day of the week.

Chapter Three

The Structure for Effective Manifestations

To be an effective manifestor, one has to understand the basic structure of this Universe and how it operates. Put differently, one has to understand the framework for effective manifestations, and how an individual fits into this overall framework. Just as there is no need to fully understand electricity or gravity in order to benefit from these physical laws, one must still live in harmony *with* these laws. This means having a basic framework through which to conceptualize these laws and understand one's relationship to them. This framework provides a visual (or descriptive) representation of the laws, which would otherwise remain unobservable to our naked eye.

For example, I have a basic framework in my mind which states that the higher I am, the greater the amount of gravitational potential energy that is stored in my body. This convenient mental representation in turn governs my actions, and prevents me from walking off the edge of tall buildings. Living life without such frameworks in place could lead to unimaginable physical injuries. In much the same way, not having a mental framework of these Universal Laws of manifestation could cause one to take many misguided physical actions in vain, and still not move any closer to their goals. It could also cause one to move further and further away from where they want to be, or result in a whole lot of struggle and heartache. This is not because the laws are not working for us, but because we are not living in accordance *with* them.

How did we all grow up to understand the basic framework of gravity? We could have picked it up while growing up—for example, by noticing that falling off the sofa was less painful than falling out of a tree! We could have also been taught these concepts by our parents, who repeatedly warned us about the danger of leaping off high places. Eventually, we got the message through repetition, and the framework was internalized within us as a kind of internal guidance system.

However, if we do not allow our children to go through life without a basic knowledge of gravity and its dangers, why do we allow ourselves to go through our adult lives without a basic understanding of our divine nature? Again, it boils down to what we discussed in the opening chapter—we are afraid of anything that cannot be observed, and hence we deliberately avoid such topics for fear of something "dangerous" lurking in the darkness. Because of the taboo nature of such spiritual topics, these essential skills are not taught in school. In addition, the unobservable nature of these universal laws prevents us from observing clearly. Most people do not have complete awareness of their thoughts and actions, and how those relate to their outer physical conditions. As a result, they are unable to make the connection between their inner states and their outer manifestations.

The secret to effective manifestations (which is also the premise of this book) lies in helping you come up with a system to accurately visualize and mentally represent all of these Universal Laws. Fortunately, doing so is much easier than it sounds, therefore, you will be an expert in no time. However, things could be difficult in the beginning because we are so used to observing and visualizing with our sense of sight. We depend on our sense of sight to get around and to provide our bearings. However, when one is learning about tapping into these Universal Laws, we must shift into using our inner awareness. Instead of looking out for physical signposts, landmarks, and maps to guide our actions, we must instead look inward for these non-physical guideposts, which will take the form of our feelings, thoughts, and emotions.

It is not enough just to learn about these Universal Laws. One must also be aware of our relation to these Universal Laws. For example, it is not enough to simply know about gravity. We must know how gravity can affect us, and where we stand in the grand scheme of things. Thus, two things are highly crucial here. First, we must build an accurate framework of these universal manifestation laws, and second, we must understand where we stand in relation to these laws. Our understanding will not be complete without either of these two components.

Let me give you a somewhat humorous example of how someone, misinformed about the laws of gravity, might approach the subject. Suppose that you did not have an overarching framework in mind about the laws of gravity. However, you noticed that each time you fell from a tree, you were in greater physical pain than when you fell off the sofa. Because the inner connection has not been made between the concept of height and the amount of gravitational energy, you instead wrongly associate "trees" with greater physical pain and "sofas" with less physical pain. Can you now see how an erroneous understanding, such that this could cause much suffering in your life? You would be wary of going near trees, because you have built up the wrong framework in your mind.

Similarly, most people's understanding of these Universal Laws centers around the archaic and erroneous framework of rewards versus punishment. Of course, it is not totally their fault, since organized religions have been drumming this subject into our heads for thousands of years, in an attempt to keep their followers in line. What happens when we walk around with such a grossly misguided framework? We become fearful of these Universal Laws. We start becoming self-conscious, judgmental, or guilty about our desires. We start believing it is bad for us to ask for what we really want. Some people spend their whole lives operating under these mistaken beliefs and do not even stop for a moment to question the validity or resourcefulness of their accepted beliefs. While we may laugh at the person who associates trees with physical pain, walking around with misguided beliefs about these Universal Laws is no laughing matter indeed! It can make the difference between a happy and unhappy life.

The good news is that many spiritual teachers who have walked the path before us have already clearly enunciated these Universal Laws through their teachings. They too, did not invent these Universal Laws, but instead discovered it for themselves through spiritual practice. Therefore, we do not have to figure out everything for ourselves. As long as we keep an open mind, we will find that the Universe willingly reveals its innermost secrets to us. All we have to do is to be open and willing to receive the answers.

If living a happy and fulfilled life is so easy, then why do so many people suffer? If the Universe is willing to give us whatever we want the moment we ask for it, why would millions of people be living in lack and in poverty? This question is often brought up by critics of these Universal Laws, and shunned by many spiritual teachers. I grappled with the same question for many years while being on this spiritual path. However, I have realized that within the answer to this question lies great power. If you can grasp the significance of the answer to this "difficult" question, then you would have achieved much in your understanding of these Universal Laws.

A popular answer to this question is that these people have attracted these circumstances for themselves. To put it bluntly, these people "asked for it." However, such an answer hardly brings inner peace to the person who asks for it. What do you mean that the person *chose* to suffer? Why would a person *choose* to suffer when he can be happy?

A more empowering answer would be that these individuals are going through life without a proper manifestations framework in place. They have not yet realized their own power in relation to the Universe. Think about a small child who is still unaware of the pitfalls of gravity or of electricity. The child will willingly stick his wet fingers into an electrical outlet or roll off the edge of a table, sometimes to serious consequences. Does it mean that the child consciously *chose* to have such an outcome for themselves? Of course not. They were operating unconsciously, unaware of the greater laws that governed their lives and how these laws related personally to them. Similarly, individuals who choose to live in lack and limitation are unconscious individuals, not yet open to their powerful abilities. Once you are awakened to your own creative abilities as a manifestor in the center of your own Universe, you will never go back to living the powerless life ever again! Never again will you willingly give up control to an imagined power that is outside of you. These people did not ask for it. They are merely unconscious creators of their own reality.

Bob Proctor, the famous spiritual teacher from *The Secret* says that a person makes $100,000 a year not because he wants to, but because he has not found a way to make $100,000 a day. What an amazing way of bringing this message across! Once someone has advanced beyond their current level of understanding and consciousness, they will never go back to their old ways of living and acting in this world again! Once I realized how I was creating my own misery in this world, I let go of all my old negative feelings and beliefs immediately. I then had better options to choose from. Within a few weeks, my outer physical circumstances changed beyond my wildest dreams! Even I was surprised by the transformations that took place within a short time in my life. Was I scared that I would regress back into my old, worrying self as I had done many times before? Not at all—because I knew that once I advanced beyond my old level of consciousness, I would never allow myself to go back. I would never allow myself to choose that path again.

We do not make $100,000 a *day* not because it is impossible to do so, but because we do not have a framework to do so yet. After all, there are some people who **do** make that kind of money! If you spent an afternoon with them and installed the proper framework for making that kind of money, do you think you would go back to making $100,000 a year? Of course not! In the same way, this book is written to elevate your own personal consciousness.

At no point in my books do I force or coerce you into making a change. You'll find that I stay away from using scare tactics or even motivational techniques to "force" you to change for the better. Such techniques are rarely effective in creating permanent, long-lasting transformations, because they depend on your willpower, and are not based on shifts in your own level of consciousness. The right way is to shift your consciousness *beyond* what it currently is, so that you start seeing a whole new set of options emerge for you. That is when you can begin to make better and more informed choices. It is also when you know you will never go back to your old ways.

The process of change and spiritual evolution is automatic. Itzhak Bentov, the spiritual mystic and author, teaches that we are all evolving in our consciousness whether we want it or not. Mankind's consciousness as a whole is constantly evolving. Spiritual masters teach that we will all get there someday, whether we like it or not. Therefore, just the process of everyday existence alone opens our eyes to various evolutionary choices and options that exist. Each new day brings us new realizations. For some people however, this can be a painfully slow way of living. They seek to have the process of inner transformation come about faster. The good news is that you *can* speed up the process through the techniques that you will learn about in the following chapters. You can, at this very moment, choose to replace an unresourceful framework with a more effective one. Once you do so, the results in your outer world will be immediate.

Chapter Four

Tapping into Optimal Zones

In the next few chapters, I am going to gradually ease you into the process of finding your own manifestation zone, a safe haven where your deepest intentions, dreams, and desires materialize as part of your outer reality.

As we go about identifying and constructing your own unique manifestation framework, keep in mind that you will need to use your *inner* senses in this journey. Because we are dealing with timeless and space-less Universal Laws here, we must be willing to step beyond our usual physical way of understanding things. In other words, you must be willing to conceptualize and look at your world differently.

The idea of a manifestation zone is so appropriate because there is literally a sweet spot that exists for everything in your life. Think about the temperature of the room you're sitting in right now. It's not just set to *any* temperature at random. Instead, there is a sweet spot in which the temperature feels just right for you. That is the spot which you find the room to be the most comfortable for your daily activities. Also, think about how there is a sweet spot for the amount of lighting in your room. If the room is too brightly-lit, the glare keeps you from reading what is on the page or on the computer screen.

The good news is that this "sweet spot" usually occupies a fairly broad range. We usually accept a variance when we are talking about the ideal temperature of our room or the amount of light there is in the room. It does not have to be a very precise number. This is an important principle to note because you do not have to be at a particular spot all the time for things to materialize and manifest in your life. All you have to be is to be in the vicinity of the spot, within the manifestation zone itself. That's why I have chosen to call this a manifestation zone and not a manifestation spot. Once you are in the zone, that's where all the conditions are ideal for outer manifestations to happen. It is when things start to move along without any input on your part.

How did I discover this concept of the manifestation zone? As I have mentioned several times, these Universal Laws are not new. However, as I was pondering my past works and reading through the questions asked by readers from all over the world, I started to wonder if there was a better way to explain all this stuff. I realized that many questions tended to follow along the lines of, "Am I doing this right or wrong? Am I following the steps in your book correctly? I don't want to do the wrong thing and make something bad happen instead."

It dawned upon me that the approach these readers were taking was one of looking for the "right" spot. When you are always worried about doing the wrong things or finding the right actions to take, then you are looking for that one and only magical spot which you believe holds the keys to your greater good. However, as I have explained, there is no one way of manifesting. There exists an infinite number of ways through which your good can get to you, just as there is not just one single spot of light in a room. What you want to do is to get yourself under the broader pool of light.

When we worry about doing the right or wrong things, we are always looking for that single spot in the room to stand or sit. Yet there's no one single "right" place, and looking for it is like setting yourself up to find the impossible. Suppose you would like to find a reasonably comfortable place to snuggle and read your book. There's not just one single spot in your room where you can do so. Thankfully, you have a range of choices available. You do not have to worry about doing the single right action or thinking that one right thought that will trigger your physical manifestations. All you have to do is to ease yourself in the manifestation zone and let the Universe take over automatically.

When you ease yourself into the manifestation zone, you are living in line with the greater Universal Laws that sustain and support this world in which we live. You tap into a stream of energy that is greater than what your physical actions alone can accomplish, and that is when the changes you seek will happen for you. However, step outside the manifestation zone, and you will be disconnected from your power. This is not because the power does not exist, but because it is so far apart from you and there is no way you can access it. Where you are currently standing in relation to the manifestation zone makes all of the difference.

There are optimal zones that exist for everything in our daily lives. For example, there exists a physical zone in your house where you do your best work. This is the place where you are the most productive. For me, I do my best work when I am sitting at my desk in my home office. When I'm in this spot, I feel empowered. I have access to all the resources and information that I need. The spot is comfortable and it feels enjoyable to be working here. Sure, I could do the same job from my sofa in the living room, but I wouldn't be as productive. For example, I would miss my two gigantic computer screens and not have all the information I need at my fingertips.

What I just described above is a physical zone. It is a physical space in my house where I do my best work. However, when I talk about manifestation zones, I am referring to a non-physical zone that is the sweet spot for your manifestations to take place. The key difference between the two is that this is not some space where you can move yourself into physically. It is a place where you have to move yourself into, metaphysically. You have to get there in spirit, however, you must first know where this space is in relation to you.

This is an important step of the puzzle because when we talk about geographical spaces, it is easy to see how you can get there. You may be in Raleigh, North Carolina today trying to get to New York City. Sure, the physical distance between these two places may be quite considerable, but Google Maps tells you the fastest route which you can take to get there. All that is left to do is to make the journey. Unfortunately, Google Maps does not exist for our inner worlds. How do we get to our manifestation zones from where we are currently?

The key lies in creating a parallel framework which we can use to guide us in our daily manifestations. For example, how do you know when you have reached New York? Well, the signs and landmarks tell you that you have arrived. In the same way, how do you tell when you are in your manifestation zone? You need to identify inner signs and landmarks which let you know that you have arrived.

This journey that you need to make is a spiritual journey. It is a journey that you embark upon *in spirit,* and is therefore unaffected by any measure of physical and geographical distance. You can ease into your manifestation zone no matter where you are or what you are doing. You can get into this sweet spot for physical manifestation no matter your current physical state or circumstances. In fact, if you are willing to get into this manifestation zone often and stay there…then it is all that is needed for your outer circumstances to shift.

I understand that all my talk of this nebulous "manifestation zone" without clearly defining where it is, may be driving some of you crazy! However, understand that I am talking about a metaphysical concept here, which is different from our usual three-dimensional, time and space understanding of the world. That is why I have to first lay the groundwork by providing some background information before showing you how to get there.

Let's start our first journey into this elusive manifestation zone. It may be easier for you to read this whole section at once, then close your eyes and follow the instructions which you have just read. Closing your eyes is helpful in the beginning as it shuts out your sensory inputs, which may distract you from taking your inner journey. Remember that you can do this exercise from anywhere. It is best to attempt this exercise while sitting down in a comfortable place where you will not be disturbed. Eventually, you'll find that you can get into your manifestation zone from anywhere, even when your physical body is moving. For now, we want to attempt this exercise while sitting down or lying still, because we do not want our physical bearings to distract us.

The journey which you make into your inner world is done *in spirit*. This means that while your physical body remains where it is, the greater part of you has actually made a big leap. Some people look at where their physical bodies are and say, "Nothing has happened! I'm still sitting in the same chair. I'm still the same person as before." However, the *person* sitting in that chair has changed. The person sitting in that chair at the end of the exercise is no longer the same person who was sitting in that chair five minutes before. You'll find that doing these exercises often will completely change the energetic makeup of your body and how you interact with the energy field around you. You'll feel different, although your physical body will still look exactly the way it is. I would not be surprised, however, if your physical body improves and heals itself as a result of doing these exercises. We are working with energy at the most fundamental levels here, and we do so through the power of our focused minds.

Lester Levenson, who created the Sedona Method, teaches that we are unlimited beings, not limited by our physical bodies. We may move around in these tiny bodies to interact with the world around us, but our mental faculties extend far beyond that. We have greater mental faculties and abilities than we realize. The reason why our mind is so powerful is that it is not limited by physical time and space. One of the most profound concepts that Levenson taught is that we can be anywhere in an instant using just the power of our minds. We can be anywhere in the Universe. It is reported that Levenson frequently did so, and his physical body could stop functioning for days or weeks on end while he explored the outer reaches of the Universe. This is similar to what some advanced yogis can do.

The space that I am guiding you into, however, will not involve the stopping of your physical apparatus. You will still be fully conscious, awake, and alert. What I am trying to do here is to guide you to cultivate a sense of heightened awareness, such that you are aware of both the physical and spiritual aspects of your being at the same time. Once you have developed the awareness that you are an eternal, spiritual being, and that the physical part of you is just a transitory illusion, then you will also simultaneously recognize your role as an unlimited creator in this Universe. You will understand the divine nature of your being and how the ability to create has always been your birthright. You have just been unconscious to this power all along.

CHAPTER FIVE
THE THREE-SECOND RULE

B ecome aware of the space that your body is currently occupying. This is the space taken up by your physical body in this three-dimensional world in which we live. When compared to the large physical land masses of this country or continent, the physical spaces occupied by our bodies can seem insignificant indeed. However, there is something else that extends far beyond our physical bodies, and it is our spiritual consciousness. This consciousness of ours knows no geographical boundaries. Its reach is unlimited by the artificial boundaries of time and space. Put differently, our spiritual consciousness extends *beyond* time and space into a realm where there is *no* time and *no* space.

This is what Levenson meant when he said that "our minds are unlimited." We are quite literally "unlimited beings" because the thoughts we think and the emotions we feel have the power to influence energy that is far beyond the reaches of our physical bodies. That is why trying to use physical actions to create the desired conditions in your life is a very inefficient way of doing things! What you

can achieve through pure, physical action alone
is absolutely minuscule compared to what can be
achieved through the power of your aligned and
focused thought!

Why do so few people recognize this importance of working with the energy field which they
are part of? Once again, it boils down to the recur-
ring themes which we have discussed in this book.
When I press a key on my keyboard, an alphabet
instantly appears on my screen. Manipulating
the physical environment around us *seems* to be a
much faster way of effecting change in the world.
However, when I think a good thought or set an
intention, it takes a much longer time for the
physical results to show up in my physical environment. This is not to say that physical manifestations
cannot be instant, but there is often a time lag in
between (also known as the buffer of time) which
makes it *seem* as if our energetic thoughts take a
longer time to materialize. And so, most people
resort to physically manipulating the things and
the people around them.

There are two issues when we live life in such
an outer-directed manner. First, and as I have mentioned above, our sphere of influence becomes
extremely small compared to what we can do through
the power of our focused thoughts. Even if we could
somehow tap into the power of the mass media and
have our words or actions projected to millions of
people across the country, our physical influence
would still be quite limited compared to what our

unlimited mental thoughts can do. Second, trying to influence things through our physical actions or words does not guarantee that things will change in the ways we desire. Everyone has their own free will, and we can never control how anyone else chooses to think or act.

I spent the first half of my life trying to change the world around me. People who want to "change the world" do not realize the futility of their actions, for the world really cannot be "changed" in the usual sense of the word. It was only after I realized the futility of going against my physical reality that I embarked upon a serious study and application of these Universal Laws. I realized that I had always been doing the steps backwards. I was trying to change the physical manifestations and the consequences themselves. What I should have done right from the beginning was to *look within myself* and to change the *cause* of all things. When you go right to the cause—where it all begins— everything in your outer world shifts into exactly the form which you would like it to be. Eventually, you reach a point where everything in your physical reality is pleasing to you...and there is nothing more you have to change.

So forget about your outer physical reality for a moment. Forget about all the people, circumstances and challenges in your life for as long as possible. I am not asking you to ignore the pressing problems in your life, for some issues do require immediate physical remediation. However, what

I've realized over the years is that *very few* issues require our immediate physical attention. In fact, I can only recall one or two instances in my life where my immediate physical attention was needed to prevent an issue from getting bigger, and that was only because I did not do the inner work necessary to stop those unwanted manifestations before they came into my physical reality. Other than that, most of the "issues" or "problems" which we consider as urgent in our lives do not require our immediate physical attention. This means we can take our attention wholly away from them and our lives will still be perfectly fine. In fact, if you take your physical attention away from all the perceived issues and problems in your life, you'll find things starting to improve without any intervention on your part. While this goes contrary to conventional wisdom, it is actually in line with these greater Universal Laws. Our sustained attention to an issue is what perpetuates the situation in the first place. When we shift our focus elsewhere, we no longer direct the powerful stream of creative universal energy in that direction. Consequently, the unwanted situation falls away by itself.

This is an interesting exercise which you can try out for today, and preferably for the rest of your life. For each outer situation which you feel tempted to immediately react or respond to (in thoughts, words or actions), ask yourself if your immediate physical attention is needed. Let me give you two contrasting examples. Suppose someone in your family fell down

41

and grazed their knee. This would qualify as a case in which immediate physical attention is needed. You would need to dress the wound and wash it to prevent infections from setting in. However, such situations are extremely rare in our daily lives. For most other situations in our lives, you will find that an immediate response to the situation is *not* warranted. Suppose that it is the middle of the month and the thought comes up about not having enough money to pay your bills at the end of the month. This is a perfect example of a situation where your immediate physical attention is not needed. Your old response to this situation might have been to spend the whole day worrying over how you would pay your bills for the month. That is giving your immediate physical attention to an unwanted situation, and consequently, causing the powerful stream of universal energy to flow in that direction. Instead, what you want to condition yourself to do is to take your mind off the matter completely. Tell yourself, "I do not have to react or respond right now, and I am still alright. Complete peace and well-being is at the core of my being." Recognize the complete peace at the center of your being in this very moment. This unshakable peace can never be disturbed by outer circumstances.

In other words, only *do* something if your well-being is threatened in this very moment. Otherwise, take your mind completely off the matter. This way of living may seem counterintuitive at first. As you go about your day, you will meet many external circumstances that "need" changing. You may meet with unpleasant colleagues or situations and feel that you need to "do something" to correct the situation. But taking this route would be doing things the hard way. You never have to correct any situation in your life, for the Universe already sees everything as perfect. Let the Universe straighten everything out for you. Let the Universe restore everything to the state of peace and perfection for you, as it has always been. The way to do so is first to remove yourself from the picture completely. This is the true meaning of letting go and letting God.

Since I began living my life in this manner, I haven't had anything unwanted crop up that has required my immediate physical intervention. Whenever I meet colleagues or friends who behave in ways that upset me, I am able to go from feeling unhappy about the situation to letting those negative feelings go within a few seconds. I am able to do so because I recognize that the cause of all my negative feelings is from wanting to change my physical reality. I *want* them to behave in ways that will please me. I *want* things to turn out in ways that will make me happy. However, the secret of having life turn out exactly the way you want it, is to withdraw your physical attention from the unwanted aspects of your life, focusing solely on the desired aspects of your life.

All it takes is just three seconds. I call it the three-second rule. Whenever a situation (or thought) comes up that you feel tempted to immediately react to, take three seconds to pause and reflect upon whether your *immediate* well-being is threatened. Do your colleague's unfriendly demeanor and words threaten your immediate well-being? This is a trick question in itself, because nothing can ever threaten your well-being, not even physical death. You are an eternal being. Is your colleague's behavior a matter of life and death? Sure, her actions could make you immensely unhappy or make you look bad in front of your boss (and thus to hurt your career in the long run), but more often than not, it is not a matter of life and death. So what? You know better. You can let it go without giving any more unwanted, unproductive attention to the situation. If you still feel the need to react after those three seconds, feel free to do so. However, you'll find that three seconds is all it takes to build your awareness and make you realize that a choice exists in *every* situation. We always have the choice of how we want to *respond* to life, and in most cases, a non-response is the best thing. If you do the inner work necessary, you'll find yourself letting go of negative feelings and thoughts in no time.

I have devoted an inordinate amount of time and space talking about *not* responding to our immediate physical environment, because my objective for this book is to have you dwell in the manifestation zone for as long as possible. I want you to live life from the manifestation zone and

never get out of it! To do so, you'll have to understand that contrary to the physical space which
your body is occupying, the manifestation zone is
a non-physical space. It is a space that exists solely
in the spiritual dimension.

This next sentence is key to your conceptual
understanding of the framework—your physical
body is at the **intersection** of the spiritual and physical dimensions (worlds) in which you live. In other
words, your physical body is the point of presence
from which you currently perceive your world, and
it serves as the connection (bridge) between your
physical and non-physical worlds.

Put simply, imagine the physical dimension as
a sheet of paper (a flat surface) and the spiritual
dimension as another sheet of paper. Imagine the
first piece of paper suspended horizontally in the air,
and the second piece of paper suspended vertically
in such a way that it cuts through (intersects) the
middle of the first piece of paper. That intersection
(represented by a single line where the two pieces of
paper meet) is your physical body. It is the physical
and spiritual space which your body occupies. Notice
how "small" this space or line is relative to the horizontal piece of paper, which represents our physical
plane. The space occupied by our physical bodies is
minuscule compared to all the physical space there
is in the world! This diagram will be helpful for your
understanding:

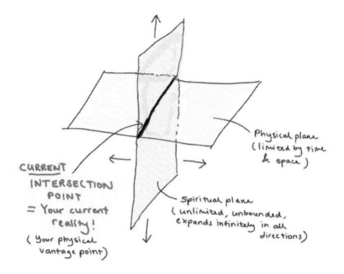

CURRENT
INTERSECTION
POINT
= Your current
reality!
(Your physical
vantage point)

Physical plane
(limited by time
& space)

Spiritual plane
(unlimited, unbounded,
expands infinitely in all
directions)

Now let's look at the spiritual dimension. Notice how thin this line is compared to the vertical piece of paper, which represents our spiritual plane. The line only occupies one thin strip on the whole piece of paper. This is our limited conscious awareness and attention. It represents all the things we are currently aware of and focused upon in our world. This analogy is powerful because it shows us that we can only devote our conscious attention and energies to a small portion of reality at any one time. The thin strip here represents our point of attraction. Whatever we focus upon here will become manifest in our physical plane, as represented by the horizontal piece of paper.

When you try to influence physical reality through outer-directed actions, your influence is limited to that single thin strip, and probably just a little bit beyond that. However, when you create reality through the mastery of these universal principles, you are able to influence the whole of reality at once. That's because you finally tap into the unlimited and infinite nature of the spiritual plane, of which you are a part. You no longer depend on the physical plane for your results. Understanding how to work on the spiritual dimension is the key to unlocking the mysteries of creation in our Universe, and it requires an extension of this powerful analogy, which we will discuss next.

CHAPTER SIX

UNLOCKING INFINITE POSSIBILITIES THROUGH THE SPIRITUAL PLANE

In the last chapter, I presented you with a framework through which you could use to visualize the nature of our Universe. We last talked about the importance of using frameworks in Chapter 3. A well-constructed framework simplifies our understanding, and provides us with a way to integrate these esoteric and unseen Universal principles into our daily lives.

Some readers may feel tempted to debate over the "accuracy" or "rightness" of these frameworks. To me, that is missing the forest for the trees. A framework is by nature a simplistic abstraction of our full reality. By constructing a framework, we are not attempting to put everything into it to construct an elaborate picture, but rather, to abstract from reality the most essential pieces of the puzzle. Therefore, the diagram of two pieces of paper intersecting in the previous chapter hardly looked like a drawing of your physical body or the world around you, but it does serve one important purpose. It allows you to visualize your role as part of the Universe. This analogy puts you right in the center of your own Universe, and shows you how you can be the creative force in your own world. Before this framework was put into place, one would have no way of visualizing how the physical and spiritual aspects of their being jointly affected their manifestations.

Now let's expand the analogy even further. The physical plane (as represented by the horizontal piece of paper) is limited in size. However, the spiritual plane (the vertical piece of paper) is literally unlimited, and extends infinitely in all directions. Think of it as a piece of paper that never ends. It stretches on and on in all directions, representing the unlimited nature of our spiritual world. This is the world that is unconfined by our traditional space-time boundaries.

Another neat feature of our spiritual world is that not only is it a very big piece of paper which stretches infinitely in both directions, it is actually many sheets of paper at once. Instead of visualizing the spiritual dimension as one single vertical sheet of paper intersecting our physical world at one single point in the middle, imagine an infinitely thick vertical stack of papers. Each piece of paper in this thick vertical stack intersects with the horizontal physical plane at a single strip. Once again, this represents the all-pervading nature of the spiritual dimension. It is omnipresent, a part of everything we do. It is present in every single aspect of our physical reality.

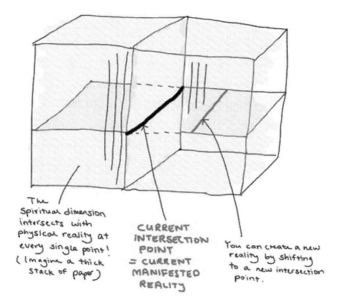

The Spiritual dimension intersects with physical reality at every single point! (Imagine a thick stack of paper)

CURRENT INTERSECTION POINT = CURRENT MANIFESTED REALITY

You can create a new reality by shifting to a new intersection point.

If one sees the spiritual dimension as God, then one could accurately say that there is nothing of which God is *not*. Other spiritual teachers have phrased it differently, by teaching that everything has a spiritual side to it, or that divine nature permeates everything in our physical reality. It is easy to see why, through this expanded framework. Since the spiritual plane intersects every single point of the physical plane and extends infinitely in all directions (there is no limit to how thick this vertical stack of paper can be), then it follows that spirit influences and is an essential part of everything in our physical world. Put differently, we can influence any aspect of our physical reality literally through our thoughts.

This framework offers you a tangible way to tap into the possibilities.

Three paragraphs ago, I asked you to assume that the physical plane (as represented by the horizontal piece of paper) was limited in size. However, if you have been following my analogy closely, then you can see that this is not exactly true. If the spiritual dimension consists of a thick stack of papers which extends infinitely in all directions and intersects with the physical plane throughout, then must be "enough" paper for the spiritual plane to intersect with. In other words, the physical plane should extend horizontally in both directions as well, like an infinitely long roll of paper. This is certainly true and conforms to our view of modern science. Physicists find that our Universe is physically expanding. In other words, while the amount of land mass on Earth is finite, the boundaries of our galactic physical Universe is constantly expanding. Our Universe is literally getting bigger each day and occupying more physical space!

What creates this expansion of our physical Universe? Let's see if you can answer this question through the use of our framework. Try to come up with an answer before reading further. That's right, the expansion of our spiritual dimension literally causes an expansion in our physical reality. But it is not only the size of our physical Universe which gets bigger, it is also the **content** of our physical reality and everything which we experience in it. This is a rather long way of saying that "thoughts become things," but I wanted to give you a tangible framework through which you can really "see" for yourself that this is so.

Most people walk around with only a nebulous idea of how they create their own reality. This leads to muddled and disappointing results. That's why most people dismiss these spiritual teachings without realizing the full power inherent in them. All spiritual teachings are designed to illustrate an important aspect of the manifestation framework you have just learned.

Let's take this saying for example: "You are made in the image and likeness of God." Most people immediately feel unworthy when they hear this saying. But if God is the whole of the spiritual dimension as represented by that infinitely thick stack of paper, then your physical body is one thin strip where two pieces of paper (one vertical and one horizontal) intersect. Would you say that this strip is "any less paper" than the thick vertical stack of papers? That would be absurd! It is made of the same paper, alright. Yet most people deny their connections to the spiritual dimension and refuse to think of themselves as part of it. The late Dr. Wayne Dyer used to say that one drop of water from the ocean contains the same properties as the entire ocean, and we can see it very clearly with this framework.

Here's where things really start to become exciting. Our physical influence is limited precisely because of the traditional boundaries of time and space. To get to anywhere else on the physical plane, one needs to travel using their physical apparatus. The physical journey therefore takes time and physical effort. Therefore, to get to somewhere else on that horizontal piece of paper, one needs to physically move their bodies there.

However, there is a far more efficient way of doing things, and that is by working through the spiritual plane. In fact, working through and in the spiritual dimension is the only way which you can unlock the infinite possibilities of our Universe. All the miracles that the great spiritual masters have worked and all the manifestations that you desire can only be realized by understanding the laws of, and working through the spiritual dimension. It is easy to see why, since our physical limitations are inherent on the physical plane. On the spiritual plane however, there are no limitations. The only limitations are self-imposed, and those which we have come to identify so closely as being a part of ourselves.

Let's talk about what you need to do to become an effective manifestor. You already know that hauling your physical body around and attempting to use it to influence people, events and circumstances is an extremely inefficient way of doing things. There only so much physical effort which you can exert before exhausting yourself. However, the greater part of you is also eternally connected to the spiritual dimension. As such, while the thin strip of paper represents the *intersection* between your physical and spiritual world and hence the manifestation of your physical body…you are *not* confined to that space. You can be anywhere else at any time *in spirit.* This is the most important part of these teachings.

First, you can place your conscious attention on anything that is *not* that intersection point between your physical and spiritual worlds. This, by itself, is quite difficult and takes some training in order to do. Most of us have identified so closely with our physical bodies and immediate physical surroundings that we see ourselves as a physical being only. Doing so would present a misguided view of the world, since I have shown through the framework that we are so much more than that. There are still aspects of our being of which we are unaware, but this does not mean that they do not exist. The secret is that most people automatically place their conscious, waking attention on that thin strip of intersection between their physical and spiritual worlds. This is only productive if what is there already pleases and delights you. But for many people, what is there does not please them. In fact, it scares them, worries them, and makes them immensely unhappy. They may look at their bodies and worry about their health. Or they may look at their finances and worry about how they will make ends meet. As a result, because their conscious attention is constantly on their observed physical reality (that thin intersection strip), the intersection point stays fixed and they are unable to effect desired changes in their lives.

Let's suppose that this individual learns about the possibility of placing their attention somewhere else. Sure, their intersection point may be somewhat unpleasant and undesirable at the moment, but they have learned not to place their attention there. They read a self-help book which talks about the power of visualization. When one visualizes, they are imagining something which they would like to manifest in their own lives. Suppose that this individual goes to the showroom and checks out a new car, and then goes on to visualize that new car, in their possession. Do you see what just happened here? The new car represents something that currently exists *on a different point* in physical reality. It occupies a *different place* on that horizontal piece of paper, that is *not* currently the intersection point. Through visualizations, this individual learns to shift his conscious attention to that *new point* on the horizontal piece of paper. By placing his attention there long enough (and without any resistant thoughts), his point of intersection will soon shift. His spiritual and physical worlds (the two pieces of paper) will soon intersect at that *new* point, and the new car becomes a reality in his own life. This is true for anything else you may ask for in your life.

Let's take this a step further. Do the things or conditions you visualize have to be anywhere in the physical world? Do they have to be anywhere on that horizontal piece of paper? Absolutely not! What you visualize does not have to exist at present in physical reality, although there is a very good chance that it already does (since someone else has already focused it into existence). But this is a very powerful concept, so stay with me here. What you focus upon can also be something anywhere in the *spiritual* plane. You can focus on something on that vertical piece (or pieces) of paper and the intersection point will still shift for you.

One good example of this is manifesting good physical health. Let's suppose that what lies at the intersection right now is a physical condition, of which you choose to let go. Of course, since there is only one of you in the physical world, you cannot go to somewhere else in the physical world to observe a perfectly healthy copy of yourself. Therefore, this perfectly healthy version of yourself has to exist somewhere on the spiritual (non-physical) plane. It exists at a certain point on the vertical piece of paper. Now, if you understand the sheer power behind these teachings and focus there, then that is where the new intersection point *has to happen*. It cannot be any other way. What you have just done is to bring something which previously did not exist in the physical world into physical reality.

Another good example is the process of inventing something new. What the inventor does is focus on something that previously only existed in their mind (the spiritual dimension). Through continued focus and inspired physical action, this object which used to exist solely in the spiritual dimension becomes a reality in the physical dimension as well. The point of intersection has thus shifted for the inventor. The invention now exists *both* on the physical as well as the spiritual plane. Therefore, learning how to shift your point of intersection is the key to fast and precise physical manifestations.

CHAPTER SEVEN
SHIFTING YOUR INTERSECTION POINT

Most readers are skeptical when I tell them that these Universal Laws can be used to create *anything* which they desire in their lives—with absolutely no exceptions. These people usually say, "Oh, these techniques are interesting, but they do not apply to this situation in my life."

If you have studied the framework which I presented in the last chapter, you'll realize the fallacy of such a statement. Why should this framework not apply to a particular situation or area in your life? Why would those sets of circumstances in your life be unchangeable? What makes them so special or different from all the other things which can be "changed" in your life? Understand that the Universe does not discern between the content of your desires. There is nothing easier or more difficult for the Universe, although we often make these distinctions ourselves and believe in them strongly. To the Universe, everything is one and the same. It is all just energy, existing as another point in the spiritual or physical dimension. Why should one point be any different from the rest? It is all just divine energy (all paper in our earlier analogy) permeating every single point in our energetic Universe. Therefore, all it takes is a simple *shift* of your intersection point and your outer reality changes accordingly.

Most people live their lives without being conscious of where their intersection points are. This is why they keep getting the same, often unwanted results in life. For them, their point of attraction equals their intersection point. They place their full attention on what has already manifested and what can be observed in their physical reality. It is therefore no surprise that they keep attracting the same-old, same-old! While they would very much like things to change in their life, they do not keep their focus on these desired conditions long enough to create a new intersection point. Instead, most people yield to the immediate influences of their outer reality. They allow what they observe through their five senses to dominate much of their conscious awareness, fueling their thoughts and emotions. These people live their lives without realizing the creative powers inherent in them, yet they are ironically creating their own reality in every moment. By allowing their current intersection point to be the same as their point of attraction, they are creating the same, often unwanted circumstances over and over again. Then, after all these unwanted conditions have manifested, these people look outside of themselves for that godly being who can help them undo all these problems in their lives, not realizing that the power to change things has always been within them.

A humorous parallel to this situation would be familiar to all parents. You are watching your young child play, and all of a sudden—a loosening of his grip causes the toy he was holding in his hands to fall to the ground and hit his toes. The pain quickly becomes apparent. He cries while looking at you, hoping that you can do something to take the pain away! As a loving father or mother, what would you do? You would recognize that the pain was not caused by anything external, but instead by your child's loosening of the grip on his toy. You would go over, rub the area lovingly and assure him that every-thing is alright. Note that while you feel love and compassion for him, there is nothing you can do to take the pain away. If he were to drop the toy on his toes again, he would experience the same pain again. Fortunately, the child soon makes a mental connection between the two and stops doing it.

We have exactly the same relationship with God, who knows and fully understands the pain we are feeling. Yet God also knows that our pain does not come from something external, no matter how things may look. It always comes from a choice we have made. God knows that the power to undo any unwanted situation always lies within us.

My purpose for writing this series of books is to help you step out of that automatic, default zone where you create, unconsciously. My intention is to

help you become a deliberate and conscious creator, where most of the things in your outer reality please you. When you find the courage to apply
these techniques on a broad range of situations
in your life, you'll find that they do indeed work
for everything. There are no exceptions. I have
experienced spiritual healings, a transformation of
relationships, financial abundance, physical manifestations of material objects, and so much more.
That's not because I am a better "manifestor" than
the next person, but because I have applied these
teachings consistently to more situations and I've
studied them more than the average person has.
You must make the conscious effort to become a
deliberate creator.

Human beings are born with innate abilities to
navigate the spiritual, non-physical dimension. I call
this the inner dimension. We gradually lost these
abilities over time as we developed a more outer-
directed way of living. Advancements in modern
technology (such as the cell phone and wireless
communications) and in the sciences has caused us
to place our entire emphasis on manipulating the
physical world around us. While this has brought
about immense improvements to our living stan-
dards, we have also brought ourselves much misery
through the misunderstanding of these Universal
Laws. The good news is that just because we have
forgotten does not mean that these abilities are
lost upon us forever. These spiritual abilities still lie
latent within us, just waiting to be activated by the

right knowing and the right intentions. They never left us in the first place.

I see this as a natural progression in the evolution of mankind. The last two hundred years have seen rapid advancement in the sciences through an emphasis on rigorous empirical measurements. Yet a new movement is also emerging. We see more people from all walks of life becoming interested in the technology of inner consciousness. There are more mass market books now on how our thoughts can change our lives and affect our health. We see corporate executives embracing the art of mindfulness, and even more scientific research conducted in these traditionally esoteric areas. I see this as a gradual discovery of the latent abilities that lie within all of us, and predict a huge explosive growth in this area over the next few decades or so. When we finally get there and use both our physical and spiritual abilities in a complementary manner, we will have come full circle. Mankind's consciousness will have then evolved to a new level.

The wonderful news is that you are at the cutting edge of this exciting change in our planet's consciousness. By reading this book, you are one of the front runners in this movement. There is no need to wait for the rest of the world to catch up before you can do any of this. You can be one of the first to experience all of these techniques and lost teachings for yourself. I often teach that I have not discovered something new. In fact, I merely adapted and synthesized these techniques from the age-old teachings of the old spiritual masters. When one recognizes the boundaries of modern science and is willing to work around them, the Universe reciprocates in the most amazing way.

Let's revisit our earlier analogy. No one has really taught us how and where to focus our thoughts. Most people live their whole lives without realizing that their points of attraction can be somewhere *other than* their intersection point. Because of their lack of this crucial piece of knowledge, they are unable to create reality in a way that truly pleases them. But you now know better. Through the previous few chapters, you know that your mental awareness can be projected to absolutely any point you want on the spiritual plane. You also know that if you keep your mental awareness there for long enough, then current reality must shift and a new intersection point must be created.

But there is still one final missing piece of the puzzle which I have not placed much emphasis on until now. I alluded to this in the first chapter, but it is at this point that our theoretical understanding is complete. This missing piece of the puzzle is *you*. You direct an unlimited, forever renewable stream of energy, by choosing what to focus your "thin strip of attention" on. Let me say that again: **You** have the volition to direct an unlimited, forever renewal stream of energy and to place that energy on absolutely anything which **you** want. This is a huge responsibility, and it is also the same source of divine energy that the ancient spiritual masters used to create miracles in their worlds.

My study of spiritual masters throughout the ages has taught me one thing. First, they dwelled almost entirely in the spiritual dimension, seeing their physical world as only a temporary dwelling. Therefore, most spiritual masters couldn't care less about what happened in the physical world or about what they possessed in this world. That's because each of them understood that our physical conditions are a mere reflection of our inner spiritual world, which is where everything begins. A few of these spiritual masters chose to temporarily dwell in the physical dimension out of sheer necessity. For example, it was necessary to make physical references and remain connected to the physical realm in order to reach out to those whom they were trying to teach. But you can imagine what a huge undertaking this would be. It requires tremendous willpower to remain focused on something which you have absolutely no interest in and know to be an illusion.

I am not asking that you give up the physical dimension and all of your material comforts immediately—that would be too big of a jump. Instead, what you want to do is to gradually shift more and more of your focus to the unseen spiritual dimension. Recall that the spiritual dimension intersects with the physical world at absolutely every single point. As such, there is a spiritual side to every physical phenomenon in this world. It helps that you remind yourself of this truth often. While out walking in the park or even at your workplace, consciously remind yourself of the fact that there is a deeper spiritual reality underlying (intersecting with) everything which you can observe with your physical senses. For example, as I look at the table upon which I'm resting my wrists, and I consciously remind myself that it is not *just a table*. This table also exists in the spiritual realm as pure energy and pure divine substance. As I look at my filing cabinet, I remind myself of the same. The filing cabinet is made up of divine energy and divine substance. When I see the people around me, I remind myself that they are spiritual beings just like myself and everyone else, and that all I am observing is an extremely limited part of who they really are. I am only observing their intersection points, the physical part of their being.

This is more than just a mental exercise. If you do this consistently over the next few weeks and months, two things will happen: First, you will internalize the framework and make it part of your being. Second, you will find your conscious awareness gradually expanding. You will find that it is impossible to look at something without also seeing its spiritual side. You will start to understand that beyond the mere physical phenomenon which you are observing exists a whole new spiritual dimension which has been closed off to you before now. You are only now starting to perceive the existence of this spiritual dimension that is eternally connected to the physicality of all things. That is when you are ready to make the shift to any point you like on the spiritual plane and to see your reality transform before you.

Chapter Eight

The Subtle Difference that Creates All Your Results

The ability to shift our intersection point is an innate human ability that has been gradually lost through the ages. The reason is because we identify so closely with our physical bodies that we find it impossible to observe and perceive life from any other point. Therefore, in order to start shifting your intersection point, one has to make an *inner* journey that is denominated in non-geographical terms. Physical travel involves outward motion. Starting from where you are physically, you move to another point on the physical plane. However, the neat thing about spiritual travel is that your physical body can remain wherever it is while your *mental* focus goes someplace else! You can do this no matter where you are, and no matter what your physical circumstances are at the moment. The ability to cultivate your inner world independent of your outer circumstances is the reason behind your amazing creative abilities.

How does one begin to navigate the inner world, and hence, shift their intersection point? It would be difficult to travel anywhere on the physical plane without a map. The same holds for the spiritual world as well. You need a roadmap to guide you. Fortunately, that roadmap exists in the form of the analogy we referred to in the past few chapters. Notice that the spiritual dimension is vast and infinite. It stretches and expands outwards in all directions. There are infinite points, infinite possibilities, and infinite solutions. Each of the points in the spiritual dimension represents a solution point where what you want exists. Therefore, if the solution, circumstances, or conditions you are looking for do not exist at the current intersection point (where you are currently), all you need to do is to shift to another point in the spiritual dimension where it exists. And since there is an infinite number of points in the spiritual dimension (which is to say, you can be anywhere on any piece of paper representing the spiritual realm), the solution you seek will always be available to you. This is the beauty of the spiritual realm.

The starting point to solving any "problem" in life or to manifesting anything you want in life is to *know* that whatever you seek exists somewhere in the infinite field. Therefore, you start with the knowing that what you are looking for already exists. There is no question about that. This may not always hold true in the physical realm, however. For example, you may want something that has not been invented yet, or something that has not yet materialized into physical form. As such, your solutions may be limited in the physical world. This is another reason why we should not place our reliance on the physical world for our answers, for not all answers to the questions we ask are there. On the contrary, we can place our full reliance (faith) in the spiritual dimension, because everything we seek is there. This is Universal Law. Since the spiritual dimension is unlimited and infinitely expansive, then whatever we ask for must exist at some point in the spiritual dimension. The infinite nature of the spiritual dimension means that it encapsulates everything we can possibly think of and ask for.

This is another reason why having a proper framework is so immensely helpful. In the past, when spiritual teachers taught that the spiritual dimension is the "source of all our supply," you may not have believed them. When they taught that "our supply is unlimited" or that "it is the Father's good pleasure to give us the kingdom," you may not have seen the literal truth behind those words. But the framework helps to put everything into perspective. You can now clearly *see*, with the help of the framework, that all these sayings are true. Not just in a figurative sense, but in the most literal of ways. The spiritual dimension *has to* be the unlimited source of all our supply because it lays beneath the surface of all physical phenomenon, and infinitely expands in all directions. Physicists have confirmed this through their discovery of our expanding physical Universe.

The most exciting discovery is that *you* can get to any point you want in the spiritual realm. You do so through your inward mental focus and attention. Since you are making use of the dichotomy between your physical presence and where you place your non-physical attention, your physical body will still remain in the same place while your inner awareness shifts. While it may seem as if nothing is happening, that is in fact when *everything* is happening. I have experienced that a few minutes each day is all you need to shift your current intersection point.

Start by closing your eyes and sitting down in a quiet and comfortable place where you will not be interrupted for the next few minutes or so. Remove any sources of distraction from your immediate physical environment, but also know that any time you are interrupted, you can simply attend to the interruption and return to what you were doing. There is no hurry or rush here. All we are doing is attempting to expand our spiritual awareness. Close your eyes and first remind yourself of the spiritual truth that the perfect solution for your issue (or the perfect manifestation which you seek) exists somewhere out there in the spiritual dimension. It is not your job to find it or know exactly where it is, but all you need is an awareness that it *exists*. It is there. It is the Universe's job to bring it to you.

This is very helpful if you are facing situations which are perceived as dead ends. You may think you are trapped by your current circumstances, and that there is nowhere to turn. You may be at your wits' end. However, this is only your current *physical* reality. There is nowhere to turn on the *physical* plane. However, a solution *always* exists on the spiritual plane, and you can count on it. Similarly, what you are trying to manifest already exists somewhere on the spiritual plane. You just have to make a connection with it, and bring it into being on the physical plane. There is nothing "rocket science" or mystical about this. Our ancient ancestors and even some indigenous tribes in various parts of the world—people whom we consider primitive and backwards—use precisely these kinds of techniques to bring what they want into physical form. We are merely reconnecting with a long lost way of living.

As you close your eyes, gently bring the awareness of the problem or issue to your mind. If you are trying to manifest something, bring your conscious awareness to what you are manifesting. Note how this represents your current intersection point. You are, at this very moment (with eyes closed), sitting squarely at the intersection point between your physical and spiritual worlds. Why is that so? Anytime we observe or perceive an issue the way things are, we line up our two worlds. We are observing from our physical perspectives and seeing things as they currently are. Anytime you think of or ponder your problem, you are bringing yourself to the current intersection point, and hence manifesting more of the same circumstances. While you may be thinking about ways to solve the problem, the very act of mulling over an issue brings you right to the intersection point, and therefore perpetuates the issue. This is perhaps the most counterintuitive part of these teachings. It is also the reason why so many people find it so difficult to shift their own realities. They just can't stop thinking about their "problems."

You'll often find me referring to "problems" or "challenges," with the words set in quotation marks. That's because they are not really problems once you understand the true nature of our Universe. How can something be a permanent problem if a solution *always* exists somewhere out there in the spiritual dimension? If there is always a spiritual solution to every problem, then does the problem even exist in the first place? Any problem in the world will at best be temporary. Therefore, your current conditions are transitory.

As you gently bring the issue you are dealing with to your conscious awareness, observe the issue without trying to solve it. The mind always conjures up possible solutions or tries to go deeper into the problem whenever it is confronted with something it sees the need to solve. The ego always sees the need to keep us safe through all sorts of mental tactics and preparatory planning. However, remember that anytime you even attempt to "solve" a problem, you are entangled with it and hence feed more energy into it. You are shifting your point of awareness to the intersection point, which leads to a perpetuation of the same outer conditions. This is a crucial point which you must understand.

The purpose of observing an issue without trying to solve it is to adopt the stance of a neutral observer. Although *observing* an issue still means feeding *some* energy into the situation, it is already a vast improvement over actively worrying about the situation. Notice how it feels to observe an issue without getting mentally involved in it. This is the starting point of your journey. It is where you are currently in the spiritual dimension, and it is from here that we will move to someplace else.

We are now going to make the journey *in spirit.* I emphasize this because your physical body is going to remain where it is, which means your physical conditions are going to remain the way they are *at least for the present.* As such, it will be misleading to use physical signs and conditions as road-markers for your inner journey. These physical markers simply do not apply here. Relying on them will mean you are reverting back to observing reality from your current intersection point.

With your eyes still closed, gently intend on moving to another point in the spiritual dimension. Remember that this is a journey made in *spirit.* No effort or force is necessary. No willpower is needed to get there. All you need to do is to set a very light intention to move, and you will be there. A good analogy for this is when you are in a dream state. In your dreams, no effort or will is needed. You simply intend to move somewhere or to do something, and it is done. It is the same kind of effortless-ness which we are talking about here. Do not *force* yourself to move, just *intend* for it to be so.

For a start, it is sufficient to move your mental focus *away* from the current intersection point (e.g., the way things currently are). Any point that is different from your current intersection point will result in a new point of attraction, and hence attract a new reality. This means that you drop the initial problem or issue from your mind entirely. How would you know when you are observing from a different point? That's when the issue, which you originally held in your conscious awareness, completely disappears into the background. You forget about it completely. You just effortlessly let it fade away. That's when you know you have moved to some place *other than* the original point. If the issue still occupies your attention or seems very stark from your current awareness, you know that you are still placing some focus on it.

With your eyes closed, feel the difference between observing from your current point of intersection (where the issues or conditions in your life seem very salient to you) and from a point *other than* your current intersection point. Feel how all your thoughts and negative emotions about the situation just seem to fade away into the background when you are at this alternate point. This crucial difference in your inner state serves as an important road marker for the rest of your journey. It lets you know whether you are pedalling at the same spot (and hence perpetuating the same circumstances in your life) or creating something new. This subtle distinction in inner feeling makes all of the difference in your outer results, which is why we will come back to this reference point as we practice these teachings.

CHAPTER NINE
ENGINEERING THE SHIFT

The only question you should ask when faced with any undesirable situation in your life is this: *Am I focused on my current intersection point (my current reality) or somewhere else?* If the answer is that you are focused on the former, then it is probably a good idea to shift that continued focus somewhere else. Any time you focus on your current intersection point, you will continue to attract and perpetuate more of the same (unwanted) conditions. There are no two ways about it. As Abraham-Hicks puts it, you cannot continue to talk about something unwanted in your life and hope that it does not come true. This is Universal Law at work here.

Fortunately, you already know the difference between attracting from your current intersection point and from an alternate point, *other than* the intersection point. This subtle difference is going to come in handy here. I will first walk you through the steps to do this technique with your eyes closed, before showing you how to apply them as you go about your daily lives. Once again, gently close your eyes and relax your body into a comfortable position.

Remember that no matter the outer circumstances or issues you're facing, they are nothing more than your temporary physical reality. Your physical reality can be shifted and changed at any time. The only person who can plant the seed for change is you. Only you have the power to decide where your new intersection point will be.

As you close your eyes, the details and awareness of the situation will naturally occupy your consciousness. However, you do not want to be entangled with the specifics of the situation here. All you want to do is to recognize that by thinking about the problem in any way or form, you are bringing yourself to the current intersection point (and therefore creating from this point). Remind yourself that the ideal outcome which you seek exists in this situation, just as it exists in every other situation. It is somewhere out there in the spiritual dimension, and you simply have to get yourself connected with the ideal outcome.

With this realization, set a very light intention to shift your mental focus somewhere *other than* your current intersection point. Take this journey *in spirit*. The way to do so is by gently thinking of shifting your inner spiritual awareness somewhere else. Remember that just as in a dream state, all you have to do is to think it, and it is done! Therefore, there is no force, struggle, or extra effort needed here. There is no trying at all. Just think that it is so. Some of you may find it helpful to vocalize the intention: "I now shift my inner awareness away from my current intersection point." Or, you may find it useful to have the visual framework in your mind, and visualize traveling from that intersection point to somewhere else on the spiritual plane.

Where you travel to does not matter. The first step is to stop creating from your current intersection point, which means to stop observing from it. As you shift your inner focus away from the current intersection point, you'll notice a few things. While your physical body still remains in the same place, your inner state has changed. Suddenly, all of the specifics of the issue which were in your mind a few moments ago have gently faded into the background. You know they were there a moment ago, but you can't seem to access them from your current state of awareness. Just notice their absence without once again trying to bring them into focus. It's like looking through a camera lens which is out of focus, and just knowing that a particular object is there. Yet somehow, you just can't get the object into focus. It is a blurry mass of colors.

As you sit there in your relaxed state, unable to recall the specifics of your issue, rest in the satisfying knowledge that you have managed to shift your inner awareness to somewhere else on the spiritual plane. Congratulations! This is probably the first time you have done so. For many people, this will be the first time in their lives when they are not actively observing and creating from their current intersection point. They have finally broken the cycle of unwanted manifestations. Then it is time to try the next step.

While keeping your breath and posture relaxed, mentally set an intention to be in touch with the ideal solution or outcome, knowing that it already exists somewhere in the spiritual dimension. All you have to do is to set an intention to get in touch with it. Remember: just think it, and it is done! Once again, all of this is done with your physical body still in its original place—but the most wonderful thing is that we are making an inner journey *in spirit* here. This journey happens instantaneously, so do not mistake physical inaction as Universal inaction. This inner exercise which you are doing has the power to move worlds and is the equivalent of thousands of hours of physical activity. You are giving up your old ways of operating in this world. No longer are you struggling to achieve something through physical action alone, but rather, you are tapping into the immense powers of aligned mental awareness. This allows you to harness your immense Universal powers of creation.

As you set an intention to be connected with this ideal outcome (whatever it may be), refrain from using any force to conjure up any images of an ideal outcome. This is not an exercise in using your imagination. We are not visualizing, or making up mental pictures for your mind here. Instead, we are setting a light intention to be taken to that ideal point on the spiritual dimension where the issue does not exist, because the solution has already unfolded perfectly. This is the desired new reality which you are creating.

Just as the specifics of your issue faded away a few moments ago, you may find feelings of peace, joy and elation start to occupy your inner awareness. Let these feelings expand and grow in their intensity. These feelings are not accidental. They did not just come out of nowhere. They are tangible signs that you are now focusing on a different point in the spiritual dimension and hence creating a whole new reality for yourself. Congratulations once again—for you have managed to get in touch with your ideal outcome.

You do not have to know what the specifics of this ideal outcome will be. Do not struggle or strain to find it. Our job has never been to worry over the small details or the "hows." Let the Universe guide and bring you to them. Let the Universe present the path of least resistance to you. Your job has always been to decide what you want and focus it into being. That has been your one and only responsibility as a conscious creator since the beginning.

Some readers are going to think that it is not enough for them to merely focus on their ideal outcome in this manner and just "do nothing." This illusion that they are doing nothing stems from their perceived physical inaction and the perceived stickiness of their physical conditions. We have been so conditioned to believe that nothing is happening when nothing moves in our physical environment. However, you have to let this old way of thinking go here. You are making immense progress in the spiritual dimension while keeping still in the physical world. Everything is shifting beneath where you are, but you lack the proper physical senses to perceive it.

With your eyes closed, continue to immerse yourself in the wonderful feelings of peace, joy, and elation that fill your inner awareness. As you rest your inner focus on these feelings, they will continue to grow and intensify. You will feel an expansiveness in your being, as if your physical presence is filling up the room you are in, and then your house, your building, and the whole of your neighborhood. This feeling of expansion is a tangible sign that you are making great spiritual progress. You are making this journey in non-physical, non-geographical terms, and you are there.

One possible temptation at this point will be to start trying to "solve" the problem and to logically think through all the possible options or solutions with your rational mind. You may believe that you should work to uncover the solution logically, since you are already at a different point on the spiritual dimension. Guess what? Doing so takes you right back to where you first began, right back to the intersection point where the problem exists. You must resist the temptation to solve the "problem" for yourself, no matter how great it is or how pressing the problem seems. Anytime you involve yourself in figuring out the specifics of the solution by thinking through the possible options or action steps, you are entangling yourself with the problem, and *not* the solution. This is a crucial difference.

What you want to do is to stay at this alternative solution point for as long as possible, and let the solutions show up themselves. You want a solution to be presented to you automatically, and this is something that cannot be forced. I've had my ideal outcome materialize in several ways, but I could never predict how my ideal outcome would manifest for me.

There are two possible ways through which manifestations can happen when you use this technique. The first way is that getting in touch and shifting our inner awareness to an alternative point on the spiritual plane connects us to completely new information which was previously out of reach for us. This new information matches our new vibrational frequency, and would never have been available to us at our old vibrational point of attraction. Since the Universe is not constrained by any physical space-time boundaries, the transmission of this information is instantaneous. I've had several encounters where flashes of ideas and insights entered my conscious awareness. These ideas and insights were things which I have never considered before, and were so far off from my logical way of thinking—I could not possibly have conjured or thought them up in any way. That's when I know I have received valuable ideas "from the void." These ideas have since been turned into business, research, and even ideas for this series of books. These flashes of insights may either come to you while you are actively engaged in this exercise with your eyes closed, or afterwards when you are going about your daily activities. Either way, you would have received inspirational guidance from the Universe.

The second way is when conditions just straighten themselves out on their own without your active physical intervention. Once again, the principle behind this is the same. When you focus from a new spiritual point of attraction, you soften your focus on current physical reality and this shifts your physical reality in a powerful way. Your intersection point changes. When you open your eyes and resume your daily activities, you may find signs indicating that your physical reality has shifted, and the conditions may continue to change over the next few days or weeks. For example, I may find that an issue that has been bothering me has straightened itself out. It no longer needs my active intervention. The other party may have suddenly changed their mind, or an opportunity becomes available to me. In my experience, this happens very frequently, and there is good reason why this is so. The Universe knows of infinite pathways to our good. If left on its own, it can orchestrate and deliver our desired outcome in the most straightforward and harmonious way possible. Very often, we are the ones preventing ourselves from moving forward through our intrusive worrisome and negative thoughts. When we observe from an alternate point in the spiritual dimension, we no longer create from the crutches of our past limiting beliefs. This is when the magic and miracles are free to happen.

How long does it take to create amazing trans-formations in your life? You may think you need to sit through the above exercise for hours on end each day in order for your physical reality to shift. Fortunately, that is not the case. It is much easier to manifest and to create your own desired version of reality than you think. All you need is just to spend five to ten minutes each day on the above steps. If you feel inspired to, close your eyes and focus on an alternative point in the spiritual dimension three times each day, for five to ten minutes each time. Since the Universe does not operate under any space or time constraints, how much time you spend actively doing these exercises is a non-issue. What matters is how well you shift your focus point and start redirecting the flow of energy to your new and desired intersection point. If you are able to take a light and playful approach to this, then you may find that change happens in an instant.

CHAPTER TEN

A RADICAL WAY TO MANIFEST 24/7

This is the final chapter of the book—where everything comes together. We have gone through a fulfilling journey together. First, I explained the importance of having a manifestations framework to visualize these Universal Laws, which would otherwise remain unseen and untapped. Next, I gave you a simplified but powerful framework to tap into these laws. A proper framework allows you to develop a moment-by-moment awareness of where you are in relation to these Universal Laws. Third, we walked through a powerful exercise which can be used to soften your focus on current reality and shift your intersection point within a very short span of time.

In this chapter, I would like to talk about a radical way to manifest 24/7. That's twenty-four hours a day, and seven days a week. In fact, just like everyone else, you *are* already a 24/7 manifestor. But much of this manifestation may be done unconsciously, without a proper knowledge of these Universal Laws. As you already know by now, if you react to life based on what you observe in your everyday reality, then you end up creating by default. You end up perpetuating the same conditions that you are trying to change. Becoming a 24/7 manifestor means recognizing the immense Universal power which you have at your fingertips, and making the greatest use of each moment to create deliberately.

The techniques I'm about to share with you are an extended version of the exercise in Chapter 9. You'll be able to apply these techniques anywhere, regardless of where you are or what physical activities you are engaged in. The secret to becoming a conscious and effective manifestor is this: you have to keep the manifestation framework in your mind at all times. As you go about your day, you physically interact with the people and things around you in your physical environment. However, an awakened manifestor knows that reality is more than that. As he moves through the day, he does not see himself as merely moving through a physical, three-dimensional environment. He also sees himself as moving through a multi-dimensional spiritual environment, an ethereal environment that is imperceptible to the physical senses.

As you move throughout your day and meet with the people and things around you, remind yourself that a spiritual dimension exists. This spiritual dimension is the underlying foundation for everything which you now see in the physical world. It is the precursor of everything that is now physical. Therefore, this spiritual dimension is where everything starts and ends. Every physical manifestation first begins as energy in the spiritual dimension which is than materialized in three-dimensional form. Similarly, everything that is physical will one day re-emerge back into the non-physical. As such, living your life without acknowledging the existence of the spiritual dimension is like missing a large piece of the jigsaw puzzle. The picture will not be complete.

What you want to do, is to develop an awareness as you move through the day that something deeper exists. In time, this awareness will be omnipresent. It will always be there. However, in the beginning, you may need to consciously remind yourself (especially during challenging times of your day) that an alternate spiritual reality always exists. Cultivating this awareness is an integral step towards becoming a 24/7 manifestor, because when you finally place more emphasis on the spiritual than the physical plane, physical manifestations will happen very quickly and effortlessly for you.

As I go through my day, it has become embedded in my consciousness that there is a spiritual side to everything. I did not start out with this understanding, though. It was only through years of focused inner work and experimentation that I arrived at this understanding. As such, I do not have to consciously remind myself of this spiritual truth now. It is always a part of my perception and my consciousness. As I move through my day, I perceive the physical world with my five senses. Yet at the same time, I perceive the spiritual world with my inner senses, guided by the framework which I shared earlier.

The most powerful part of these teachings is that while your physical body is always at the intersection point between your physical and spiritual dimensions, **your spiritual awareness does not have to be.** This is key to becoming an effective manifestor. Only place your spiritual awareness at your current intersection point if what is there is something you desire. Otherwise, you are better served by *separating* your physical point of observation from your spiritual point of awareness. If you live your days with such a conscious separation, you'll find circumstances quickly changing to your liking in the physical world. Very soon, everything that is manifested in your physical environment will be pleasing to you.

Now you can see why this is an extended (and advanced) version of the exercise in the previous chapter. In Chapter 9, we only attempted to shift our inner focus with our eyes closed, while our physical bodies were still and not doing anything. In this chapter, we shift our inner focus with our eyes open, and as our physical bodies are going through its daily motions. This is not an easy thing to do initially, but it is very rewarding for someone who manages to do so.

This does not mean that you are not present in every moment. I am not asking that you become detached and unfeeling in all of life's moments. You are still fully present in your physical body, fully alive and experiencing what all of life has to offer. However, the key distinction is this: while you experience what physical reality has to offer, you are simultaneously aware of a deeper spiritual reality. At the same time, you are aware that you can place your focus on somewhere else in that physical reality. You then choose to dwell on that alternate spiritual point most of the time.

Let's suppose you go through the day and meet with a frustrating and stressful situation. Normally you would have reacted negatively and spent your day fuming about the incident. This is placing your full attention on the current point of intersection, and hence perpetuating unwanted reality. However, remembering these teachings, you recognize the deeper spiritual reality that exists. You know that somewhere out there in the spiritual realm lies the perfect outcome of this situation, a place where the problem does not even exist at all. As such, while your physical body is still at your current intersection point "observing" the less-than-favorable conditions, your spiritual awareness has shifted to that alternate point. Most of your focus is there. You now realize it is much more difficult to get angry or to react at the current situation because you are no longer *here*, you are over *there*. You have started to shift your reality with a simple shift in focus.

Now let's suppose you continue through your day and the incident keeps playing out in your mind. You find negative thoughts of worry and anger in your consciousness. I am not asking that you detach yourself from these thoughts. Acknowledge that they are there, and that you feel anger, worry, or sadness. These thoughts are based on current reality. Once again, you can choose to dwell somewhere else in the spiritual realm. Place your focus on that desired solution point and live there for the rest of the day. Separate your non-physical (spiritual/mental) awareness from your physical awareness. This is the most valuable skill which you can cultivate for yourself. It may feel unnatural or even silly in the beginning, but there is great value to this practice.

Here's an example from my own life: In my early days, I was constantly worried about not having enough money. My intersection point back then was the physical realization of lack in my bank account. However, I had not yet grasped the significance of these Universal Laws. I saw physical reality as solid and unchangeable. To me, physical reality was the be-all and end-all, the final state of all things. My misguided beliefs about the unchangeable state of physical reality made me very depressed. How was I going to change something as solid as physical reality? How could I make more money? Because of my misguided beliefs, the only way out was to attempt to manipulate the physical reality around me…to figure out more ways through which I could work and make some money. This belief that I needed to do things I did not like to do in order to make more money brought me more and more unhappy situations…and the cycle continued.

One memory that stands out from that period is that I always had a clear picture of my bank account balance in my mind. If you asked me back then what my account balance was, I could always tell you precisely, and it wasn't an amount that pleased me! It was an amount that caused me great worry as I went through my day. I spent most of my waking hours with a mental picture of my bank account balance in my mind. It is therefore no surprise that my physical reality *could not* shift! I was spending every waking hour focused on my current intersection point, observing my then-reality the way it was, and unknowingly perpetuating reality the way it was.

The fastest transformations occurred the moment I started applying the manifestation techniques I covered in this book. Of course, no one had laid them out so nicely for me in those days, so there was a lot of trial-and-error involved. However, I began to gradually loosen my focus on my bank account balance. Initially, I started to deliberately not focus on it so much. I started to place my conscious awareness somewhere else. While I still *knew* that it was a figure that worried me, I conditioned myself to stay focused elsewhere. I was unknowingly putting these Universal Laws to work in ways that benefited me. Within a few weeks, my financial situation began to shift and improve. New sources of income and opportunities started flowing to me with no active intervention on my part. However, I had to make the first move.

The first move is not always easy to make. It took a great leap of courage for me to momentarily divert my attention away from something that scared me initially. But taking my attention away did not make it worse as I had always feared. Instead, my lack of attention somehow made things *better*. A simple shift in my conscious awareness is all that was needed. I say this because some of you may be fearful to make the first move right now. I see many people asking for "proof" that this works before they are willing to give up their own self-sabotaging ways of thinking and acting in the world. But only **you** can prove these Universal Laws to yourself. You cannot depend on someone else to prove them *to* you.

I dwell mostly on the spiritual dimension nowadays. This is not to say that I do not enjoy my physical life experience. Neither am I detached from life. I still enjoy life greatly, and I cherish my interactions with everyone else. I enjoy all my nice physical gadgets and spend lots of time checking out reviews of new gadgets. But there is one important difference: the person on the inside has changed. Instead of seeing physical reality as the final unchangeable state of things, I see it as malleable and always shifting. More important, it is always shifting into something more desired for me through the application of these Universal Laws. When I see something I dislike in my physical reality, I waste no time in trying to undo things at a physical level. I go right down to the source, to the spiritual dimension where it all begins—and work from there. I direct my stream of creative energy with great care and respect.

You too, can live life in this radical way. It starts with nothing more than a willingness to give up your old erroneous beliefs about the world, and to adopt a more resourceful framework. As I mentioned, when you have believed something all your life, it may be difficult (and even scary at first) to let things go. It may be difficult to take your eyes off something that worries you a lot, for fear that the situation will get worse if you don't attend to it. Be like me, and like everyone else who has taken this path: take the first step in faith, and the rest will follow. You are the best person to prove these Universal Laws to yourself. The good news is that they work equally for everyone who works them. They will not work for someone who does not apply them and then goes around asking for proof. Prove them to yourself!

Use these powers that have always been a part of you, and immerse yourself in the spiritual dimension for longer and longer periods at a time. Initially, it may only be for five to ten minutes. Then try to stay there for hours on end, and then for days on end. Stay there for months and never come out of it. Eventually, you'll find yourself dwelling constantly on things that please you while everything unpleasant just seems to gently fade away and become a thing of your past. When you meet with unpleasant situations that stir up negative emotions, acknowledge their existence in your physical world, but take them lightly. These conditions are temporary and can be changed in an instant. Why invest your precious stream of energy into mulling over something unwanted? Let all of it go and maintain your focus on that higher reality. By so doing, you'll join a small group of spiritual masters who have realized and practiced these timeless truths for themselves.

If you will do so for the rest of your days, then you'll realize that your physical reality is not the end of everything. It is in fact, the beginning of a period of flourishing and of change in your life. But the true beginnings of everything lie in that barely perceptible spiritual dimension, just beneath the surface of your physical reality. That is where you should reside for most of the time in order to be an effective manifestor. Even if you forget all the words in this book and just *stay there*, it will be sufficient. You will have found your sacred manifestation zone, and from there, everything is done!

ABOUT THE AUTHOR

Richard Dotts is a modern-day spiritual explorer. An avid student of ancient and modern spiritual practices, Richard shares how to apply these timeless principles in our daily lives. For more than a decade, he has experimented with these techniques himself, studying why they work and separating the science from the superstition. In the process, he has created successful careers as an entrepreneur, business owner, author and teacher.

Leading a spiritual life does not mean walking away from your current life and giving up everything you have. The core of his teachings is that you can lead a spiritual and magical life starting right now, from where you are, in whatever field you are in.

You can make a unique contribution to the world, because you are blessed with the abilities of a true creator. By learning how to shape the energy around you, your life can change in an instant, if you allow it to!

Richard is the author of more than 20 Amazon bestsellers on the science of manifestation and reality creation. A list of his current books can be found at http://www.RichardDotts.com.

An Introduction to the Manifestations Approach of Richard Dotts

Even after writing more than 20 Amazon bestsellers on the subject of creative manifestations and leading a fulfilling life, Richard Dotts considers himself to be more of an adventurous spiritual explorer than a spiritual teacher or "master", as some of his readers have called him by.

"When you apply these spiritual principles in your own life, you will realize that everyone is a master, with no exceptions. Everyone has the power to design and create his own life on his own terms," says Richard.

"Therefore, there is no need to give up your power by going through an intermediary or any spiritual medium. Each time you buy into the belief that your good can only come through a certain teacher or a certain channel…you give up the precious opportunity to realize your own good. My best teachers were those who helped me recognize the innate power within myself, and kept the faith for me even when I could not see this spiritual truth for myself."

Due to his over-questioning and skeptical nature (unaided by the education which he received over the years), Richard struggled with the application of these spiritual principles in his early years.

After reading thousands of books on related subjects and learning about hundreds of different spiritual traditions with little success, Richard realized there was still one place left unexplored.

It was a place that he was the most afraid to look at: **his inner state.**

Richard realized that while he had been applying these Universal principles and techniques dutifully on the outside, his inner state remained tumultuous the whole time. Despite being well-versed in these spiritual principles, he was constantly plagued with negative feelings of worry, fear, disappointment, blame, resentment and guilt on the inside during his waking hours. These negative feelings and thoughts drained him of much of his energy and well-being.

It occurred to him that unless he was free from these negative feelings and habitual patterns of thought, any outer techniques he tried would not work. That was when he achieved his first spiritual breakthrough and saw improvements in his outer reality.

Taking A Light Touch

The crux of Richard's teachings is that one has to do the inner work first by tending to our own inner states. No one else, not even a powerful spiritual master, can do this for us. Once we have restored our inner state to a place of *zero*, a place of profound calmness and peace...that is when miracles can happen. Any subsequent intention that is held with <u>a light touch</u> in our inner consciousness quickly becomes manifest in our outer reality.

Through his books and teachings, Richard continually emphasizes the importance of taking a light touch. This means adopting a carefree, playful and detached attitude when working with these Universal Laws.

"Whenever we become forceful or desperate in asking for what we want, we invariably delay or withhold our own good. This is because we start to feel even more negative feelings of desperation and worry, which cloud our inner states further and prevent us from receiving what we truly want."

To share these realizations with others, Richard has written a series of books on various aspects of these manifestation principles and Universal Laws. Each of his books touches on a different piece of the manifestation puzzle that he has struggled with in the past.

For example, there are certain books that guide readers through the letting-go of negative feelings and the dropping of negative beliefs. There are books that talk about how to deal with self-doubt and a lack of faith in the application of these spiritual principles. Yet other books offer specific techniques for holding focused intentions in our inner consciousness. A couple of books deal with advanced topics such as nonverbal protocols for the manifestation process.

Richard's main goal is to break down the mysterious and vast subject of spiritual manifestations into easy to understand pieces for the modern reader. While he did not invent these Universal Laws and is certainly not the first to write about them, Richard's insights are valuable in showing readers how to easily apply these spiritual principles despite leading modern and hectic lifestyles. Thus, a busy mother of three or the CEO of a large corporation can just as easily access these timeless spiritual truths through Richard's works, as an ancient ascetic who lived quietly by himself.

It is Richard's intention to show readers that miracles are still possible in our modern world. When you experience the transformational power of these teachings for yourself, you stop seeing them as unexpected miracles and start seeing them as part of your everyday reality.

Do I have to read every book in order to create my own manifestation miracles?

Because Richard is unbounded by any spiritual or religious tradition, his work is continuously evolving based on a fine-tuning of his own personal experiences. He does, however, draw his inspiration from a broad range of teachings. Richard writes for the primary purpose of sharing his own realizations and not for any commercial interest, which is why he has shied away from the publicity that typically comes with being a bestselling author.

All of his books have achieved Amazon bestseller status with no marketing efforts or publicity, a testament to the effectiveness of his methods. An affiliation with a publishing house could mean a pressure to write books on certain popular subjects, or a need to censor the more esoteric and non-traditional aspects of his writing. Therefore, Richard has taken great steps to ensure his freedom as a writer. It is this freedom that keeps him prolific.

One of Richard's aims is to help readers apply these principles in their lives with minimal struggle or strain, which is why he has offered in-depth guidance on many related subjects. Richard himself has maintained that there is no need to read each and every single one of his books. Instead, one should just narrow in to the particular aspects that they are struggling with.

As he explains in his own words, "You can read just one book and completely change your life on the basis of that book if you internalized its teachings. You can do this not only with my books, but also with the books of any other author."

"For me, the journey took a little longer. One book could not do it for me. I struggled to overcome years of negative programming and critical self-talk, so much so that reading thousands of books did not help me as well. But after I reached that critical tipping point, when I finally 'got it', then I started to get everything. The first book, the tenth book, the hundredth book I read all started to make sense. I could pick up any book I read in the past and intuitively understand the spiritual essence of what the author was saying. But till I reached that point of understand within myself, I could not do so."

Therefore, one only needs to read as many books as necessary to achieve a true understanding on the inside. Beyond that, any reading is for one's personal enjoyment and for a fine-tuning of the process.

Which book should I start with?

There is no prescribed reading order. Start with the book that most appeals to you or the one that you feel most inspired to read. Each Richard Dotts book is self-contained and is written such that the reader can instantly benefit from the teachings within, no matter which stage of life they are at. If any prerequisite or background knowledge is needed, Richard will suggest additional resources within the text.

OTHER BOOKS
BY RICHARD DOTTS

M any of these titles are progressively offered in various formats (both in hard copy and for the Amazon Kindle). Our intention is to eventually make all these titles available in hard copy format.

Please visit http://www.RichardDotts.com for the latest titles and availability.

- **Banned Manifestation Secrets**
  It all starts here! In this book, Richard lays out the fundamental principles of spiritual manifestations and explains common misconceptions about the "Law of Attraction." This is also the book where Richard first talks about the importance of one's inner state in creating outer manifestations.

- **Come and Sit With Me (Book 1): How to Desire Nothing and Manifest Everything**
  If you had one afternoon with Richard Dotts, what questions would you ask him about manifesting your desires and the creative process? In Come and Sit With Me, Richard candidly

answers some of the most pressing questions that have been asked by his readers. Written in a free-flowing and conversational format, Richard addresses some of the most relevant issues related to manifestations and the application of these spiritual principles in our daily lives. Rather than shying away from tough questions about the manifestation process, Richard dives into them head-on and shows the readers practical ways in which they can use to avoid common manifestation pitfalls.

- **The Magic Feeling Which Creates Instant Manifestations**
  Is there really a "magic feeling", an inner state of mind that results in almost instant manifestations? Can someone live in a perpetual state of grace, and have good things and all your deepest desires come true spontaneously without any "effort" on your part? In this book, Richard talks about why the most effective part of visualizations lies in the *feelings*…and how to get in touch with this magic feeling.

- **Playing In Time And Space: The Miracle of Inspired Manifestations**
  In Playing In Time And Space, Richard Dotts shares the secrets to creating our own physical reality from our current human perspectives. Instead of seeing the physical laws of space and time as restricting us, Richard shares how anyone can transcend these perceived limitations of

space and time by changing their thinking, and manifest right from where they are.

- **Allowing Divine Intervention**

  Everyone talks about wanting to live a life of magic and miracles, but what does a miracle really look like? Do miracles only happen to certain spiritual people, or at certain points in our lives (for example, at our most desperate)? Is it possible to lead an everyday life filled with magic, miracles and joy?

  In Allowing Divine Intervention, Richard explains how miracles and divine interventions are not reserved for the select few, but can instead be experienced by anyone willing to change their current perceptions of reality.

- **It is Done! The Final Step To Instant Manifestations**

  The first time Richard Dotts learnt about the significance of the word "Amen" frequently used in prayers...goosebumps welled up all over his body and everything clicked in place for him. Suddenly, everything he had learnt up to that point about manifestations made complete sense.

  In It Is Done!, Richard Dotts explores the hidden significance behind these three simple words in the English language. Three words, when strung together and used in the right fashion, holds the keys to amazingly accurate and speedy manifestations.

- **Banned Money Secrets**

  In Banned Money Secrets of the Hidden Rich, Richard explains how there is a group of individuals in our midst, coming from almost every walk of life, who have developed a special relationship with money. These are the individuals for whom money seems to flow easily at will, which has allowed them to live exceedingly creative and fulfilled lives unlimited by money. More surprisingly, Richard discovered that there is not a single common characteristic that unites the "hidden rich" except for their unique ability to focus intently on their desires to the exclusion of everything else. Some of the "hidden rich" are the most successful multi-millionaires and billionaires of our time, making immense contributions in almost every field.

  Richard teaches using his own life examples that the only true, lasting source of abundance comes from behaving like one of the hidden rich, and from developing an extremely conducive inner state that allows financial abundance to easily flow into your life.

- **The 95-5 Code: for Activating the Law of Attraction**

  Most books and courses on the Law of Attraction teach various outer-directed techniques one can use to manifest their desires. All is well and good, but an important question remains unanswered: What do you do during the remainder of your time when you are not actively using these manifestation techniques? How do you live? What do you do with the 95% of your day, the majority of your waking hours when you are not actively asking for what you want? Is the "rest of your day" important to the manifestation process?

It turns out that what you do during the 95% of your time, the time NOT spent visualizing or affirming, makes all of the difference.

In The 95-5 Code for activating the Law of Attraction, Richard Dotts explains why the way you act (and feel) during the majority of your waking hours makes all the difference to your manifestation end results.

- **Inner Confirmation for Outer Manifestations**

How do you know if things are on their way after you have asked for them?

What should you do after using a particular manifestation technique?

What does evidence of your impending manifestations feel like?

You may not have seen yourself as a particularly spiritual or intuitive person, much less an energy reader...but join Richard Dotts as he explains in Inner Confirmation for Outer Manifestations how everyone can easily perceive the energy fields around them.

- **Mastering the Manifestation Paradox**

The Manifestation Paradox is an inner riddle that quickly becomes apparent to anyone who has been exposed to modern day Law of

Attraction and manifestation teachings. It is an inner state that seems to be contradictory to the person practicing it, yet one that is associated with inevitably fast physical manifestations—that of *wanting* something and yet at the same time *not wanting* it.

Richard Dotts explains why the speed and timing of our manifestations depends largely on our mastery of the Manifestation Paradox. Through achieving a deeper understanding of this paradox, we can consciously and deliberately move all our desires (even those we have been struggling with) to a "sweet spot" where physical manifestations *have to occur* very quickly for us instead of having our manifestations happen "by default."

- **Today I Am Free: Manifesting Through Deep Inner Changes**
  In Today I Am Free, Richard Dotts returns with yet another illuminating discussion of these timeless Universal Laws and spiritual manifestation principles. While his previous works focused on letting go of the worry and fear feelings that prevent our manifestations from happening in our lives, Today I Am Free focuses on a seldom discussed aspect of our lives that can affect our manifestations in a big way: namely our interaction with others and the judgments, opinions and perceptions that other people may hold of us. Richard Dotts shows readers

simple ways in which they can overcome their constant feelings of fear and self-consciousness to be truly free.

- **Dollars Flow To Me Easily**

  Is it possible to read and relax your way into financial abundance? Can dollars flow to you even if you just sat quietly in your favorite armchair and did "nothing"? Is abundance and prosperity really our natural birthright, as claimed by so many spiritual masters and authors throughout the ages?

  Dollars Flow To Me Easily takes an alternative approach to answering these questions. Instead of guiding the reader through a series of exercises to "feel as if" they are already rich, Richard draws on the power of words and our highest intentions to dissolve negative feelings and misconceptions that block us from manifesting greater financial abundance in our lives.

- **Light Touch Manifestations: How To Shape The Energy Field To Attract What You Want**

  Richard covers the entire manifestation sequence in detail, showing exactly how our beliefs and innermost thoughts can lead to concrete, outer manifestations. As part of his approach of taking a light touch, Richard shows readers how to handle each component of the manifestation sequence and tweak it to produce fast, effective manifestations in our daily lives.

- **Infinite Manifestations: The Power of Stopping at Nothing**

  In Infinite Manifestations, Richard shares a practical, step-by-step method for erasing the unconscious memories and blocks that hold our manifestations back. The Infinite Release technique, "revealed" to Richard by the Universe, is a quick and easy way to let go of any unconscious memories, blocks and resistances that may prevent our highest good from coming to us. When we invoke the Infinite Release process, we are no longer doing it alone. Instead, we step out of the way, letting go and letting God. We let Universal Intelligence decide how our inner resistances and blocks should be dissolved. All we need to do is to intend that we are clear from these blocks that hold us back. Once the Infinite Release process is invoked, it is done!

- **Let The Universe Lead You!**

  Imagine what your life would be like if you could simply hold an intention for something…and then be led clearly and precisely, every single time, to the fulfilment of your deepest desires. No more wondering about whether you are on the "right" path or making the "right" moves. No more second-guessing yourself or acting out of desperation—You simply set an intention and allow the Universe to lead you to it effortlessly!

- **Manifestation Pathways: Letting Your Good Be There…When You Get There!**
  Imagine having a desire for something and then immediately intuiting (knowing) what the path of least resistance should be for that desire. When you allow the Universe to lead you in this manner and unfold the manifestation pathway of least resistance to you, then life becomes as effortless as knowing what you want, planting it in your future reality and letting your good be there when you get there…every single time! This book shows you the practical techniques to make it happen in your life.
- **And more…**

Made in the USA
Columbia, SC
23 November 2024

47416371R00065